To Natalia Goldberg,

who titled this book for me and kept you from reading

Adrianna Cuevas Book 6

ONE

OVERCOOKED EGGS LOOK like exploded eyeballs. The yellow and white bits stick to the pan on the stove, glued to the surface because not only did I forget to spray the skillet, I got distracted by the gurgling sound of Profe's coffee maker. The bubbling and hissing noise made me think of a story I wrote about an archaeologist being dangled over a pit of acid. By the time I imagined my hero swinging from the rope tied around his ankle to safety, the smell of burnt eggs snapped me back to reality and my breakfast was beyond saving.

I pull a tortilla out of the bread box and scrape the dry, burnt yolks onto it so I can roll it up and cover my breakfast disaster in cheese. My taste buds have only wanted to eat scrambled eggs for breakfast for the past two weeks, but I think I'm finally starting to get tired of them.

"Frani, you need to soak that pan," a voice calls over my shoulder.

Maggot nostrils. Busted.

"I know," I tell my sister, Esperanza. "I got it."

I turn just in time to see her black eyebrow arch pointedly up her forehead. "Oh really?" she says. "Like you had it when you set the smoke alarm off because you forgot you put bread in the toaster? Or when you boiled over an entire pot of pasta because you weren't paying attention to it?"

I groan and wave my hand across the kitchen. "Is the house still here, Essie? Have I set anything on fire? No, I haven't, thank you very much."

At least not yet.

And it wasn't really my fault. It was Arañita, the spider that lives in my brain web. While I was making toast, Arañita scanned the living room and spotted the latest manga I'd been reading. She wanted to dive back into the world of human-robot hybrids battling sea monsters and I didn't notice the smoke snaking out of the toaster until the loud beeping alarm pulled me out of my book.

Arañita's always to blame when my brain jumps from one thing to another. She bounces along her web, hopping across the threads without thinking about where she's been or where she's going. The teachers and counselors at school tried to give my distracted brain a four-letter label, but I know the truth: it's Arañita.

I grab the skillet and toss it in the sink, the loud clatter making Profe look up from his coffee. He glances from me to Essie, tugs on the sleeve of his blue fishing shirt with too many pockets, and goes back to scrolling through his email on his phone.

"Just make sure you don't cook anything until I get back home. I don't want to get a call from the fire department." Essie crosses her arms and blows a strand of frizzy black hair off her forehead. "Don't leave the refrigerator door open again either. You'll spoil all our food. And you need to fold your laundry too. I keep losing my work uniform in the pile of mess you're ignoring."

I groan at Essie's list of chores and rules. She's still mad at me about Disaster Day, even though it was two whole months ago. That week at school, I wasn't paying attention when I grabbed my science notebook off the kitchen table and accidentally took Essie's English research paper she was supposed to turn in that day. Then I made her late to school because I missed the bus and she had to convince her girlfriend, Yaikira, to drive me to my middle school before they went to the high school.

It's not my fault Arañita decided I needed to organize my closet when I was picking out what to wear. When I tried to make it up to Essie by baking some chocolate chip cookies, Arañita kept bouncing around the steps in the recipe and I made them completely wrong.

Apparently, sisters throw up when they eat cookies

made with salt instead of sugar.

I roll my eyes. "I'm working with Profe today."

Essie's lips purse in a tight line. She hates it when I call our dad Profe. But he's Dr. Bernardo Gonzalez, senior professor and researcher at Central Texas University. I've always called him Profe, just like most of his students do. I've been going to Profe's classes ever since I was in third grade.

That year I got strep throat and had to miss a week of school. Profe didn't want me staying home by myself, so I tagged along with him to his lectures. I sat in his Introduction to Forensic Anthropology class and learned to identify how long a body has been dead, how fast it takes for muscles to decompose, and what kinds of insects like to feast on cadavers. Profe even had huge photographs of dead bodies projected on the screen in the lecture hall. Sitting in that class, Arañita was the calmest she's ever been. After that, I begged Profe to let me skip school and go to his lectures. I even faked being sick a few times until he caught on.

Over the summers, though, I don't have to convince Profe to let me miss school. We have all the time we want. So I spend my days helping him with whatever research he's doing.

"Hello?" Essie snaps her fingers in front of my face. I hate when she does that. "You're spacing out again."

"Aren't you going to be late for work?" I shoot back. Essie

has a job at Whataburger and I point at the bright orange polo shirt she has to wear. "Those Dr Pepper Shakes don't make themselves, you know."

Essie glances at her cell phone, checking the time. Even though she's seventeen, she doesn't have a car and has to wait for Yaikira to pick her up. She always walks to the gate at the edge of our property since there's so much security. And she definitely doesn't want Yaikira or any of her friends seeing what's in our backyard.

Essie turns quickly on her heel but can't resist calling over her shoulder "Don't forget to do the dishes!" as she leaves.

I shake my head, grabbing my egg tortilla disaster and sitting down next to Profe at the kitchen table. Biting into my breakfast, I wonder if it's possible for a human being to die from eating dry, burnt eggs. Does stomach acid take one look at the overcooked yolks and say, "Nope. We're sending this back where it came from." I swallow hard, trying to make sure my breakfast stays down where it should.

A chuckle from Profe snaps me from my thoughts. I look at him as he holds his coffee cup to his lips, the steam fogging up his glasses.

"Probably no chance your sister will bring home cheese and jalapeño burgers for dinner now, is there? Too bad."

Profe smiles before he takes a long sip of his black

coffee from the mug I decorated for him in fourth grade with pictures of colorful skulls, leg bones, and ribs. It's his favorite mug.

I laugh. "Did you know Venus flytraps can survive on one bug every two weeks?"

Profe sets his coffee cup down and examines my face. I know he's searching for how I bounced from him talking about Essie getting dinner to insect-eating plants. The connection made sense in my head. The jalapeño burgers made Arañita jump to spicy food, which then made her leap to thinking about the time we went to a Japanese restaurant and I accidentally ate a whole spoonful of wasabi. Arañita remembered I brought my favorite manga to read while we waited for our food, a story about plants eating people who trespass in their forest. And then Arañita landed on how Venus flytraps are carnivorous plants.

This happened in about two seconds.

Profe nods. He's used to my brain doing this as Arañita jumps all over the place. Other people aren't. My teachers think if I just try hard enough, I can focus and not daydream. And the kids at school always give me weird looks when I blurt out the random thoughts that Arañita pushes out of my mouth. Or they complain when they have to do group work with me because I focus on one tiny piece of the project and forget to do the rest of the assignment. That's why it's usually just me and Arañita by ourselves at lunch.

"Everything okay, Frani?" Profe asks. He wraps his fingers around his coffee mug, and I realize I've been bouncing my leg up and down, shaking the table in the process.

I pick at the edge of the tortilla on my plate and arrange the crumbs to spell *NO*.

I open my mouth but Profe's phone buzzes on the table. A slight smile creeps onto his lips when he reads the message.

"Well, I think today will be a good day," he says.

"Why?" I wish he'd tell me exactly what he wants to say before Arañita decides to speed past this conversation and jump along thirty threads.

"Just got notified we have an incoming specimen." Profe brushes his fingers through his black hair. "I was thinking maybe you could lead the team. You know, take over the processing."

The burnt eggs in my stomach shoot up to my throat and I swallow hard to keep them down. My leg bounces again under the table. "Really? You're serious? You're not joking? Because that would be the worst joke in the history of bad jokes."

Profe smiles and gets up from the table, setting his coffee cup in the sink next to my discarded skillet.

"I think you're ready. Why don't you give it a try?"

I jump up, almost knocking over my chair. "I can do it. I know I can," I tell Profe. I clench my hands at my sides as Arañita races past each step of the processing I'll have to complete today. I try to slow her down but it's no use. She's speeding across silk threads, ducking under webs, and skipping along thin lines.

Profe shuffles out of the kitchen to get ready. I grab my plate from the table and dump the rest of my breakfast disaster in the trash.

Before I can head to my room to find my shoes and my favorite hair tie, I hear Profe call down the hall, "Don't forget to soak that pan or your sister will scream loud enough to destroy the roof."

He's not wrong. I flip on the faucet and wait for the pan to fill up with water. Looking out the window above the sink, I gaze past the tall chain-link fence to the mesquite bushes and cacti that have sprouted up from the rocky ground.

I can almost see the small mounds in the dirt that make up Profe's research and his job.

Our house sits on twenty-six acres that are part of the university. My backyard is probably different from anyone else's at San Zavala Middle School. There's no swing set or trampoline. No deck with a grill. And definitely no swimming pool.

I squint and watch a large buzzard land on a live oak branch. It scans the ground, looking for its own tasty breakfast. I know exactly what it's going to pick. The land stretching out from the kitchen window is practically a buffet.

That's because there are two hundred and thirty-seven bodies buried in my backyard.

TWO

PROFE AND I walk from our back porch and along the winding cement path to his research building, which sits down the hill from our house. When the old caretaker of the facility retired two years ago, Profe convinced the university that it would be easier for him to complete his research and maintain security if he lived on the property. So our new home became Central Texas University's Forensic Anthropology Research Facility.

Now, instead of playing on a tire swing in my backyard, I help Profe track the decomposition of cadavers so police and investigators can better identify human remains. I guess there's worse things I could be doing. I can't think of any right now, but I'm sure they exist. Probably.

It's not like I have anyone else to hang out with anyway.

"Frani, let me know you heard what I just said," Profe says as we keep walking.

I tug on the hem of my T-shirt, the thick humidity already sticking it to my back with sweat.

"Um, repeat, please," I tell him. Arañita makes me have to hear things more than once.

Profe clears his throat. "You know there are lots of steps to processing a new cadaver. We need to make sure we do everything in the right order, okay?"

I take a deep breath. Completing things in a set order and not skipping any parts isn't easy for Arañita. My math teachers always get frustrated because I don't show every single step I use to complete a problem but I still get the right answer. Arañita jumps ahead in the process and didn't need to write everything down.

They think I'm cheating.

As Profe and I enter the research building, I reassure him that I'll do my best.

"Good morning, Frani!" Dr. Simon Tanaka, one of Profe's assistants, calls across the heavily air-conditioned room. He's been at the facility since last year, researching how different types of fabrics affect the decomposition process.

I start to greet him, but someone new is in the lab. He looks like Dr. Tanaka but about my age. He's wearing a *One Piece* T-shirt and his black-and-white Vans have a small hole over his left big toe. His eyes are huge as he looks around at the test tubes, body bags, and bleached bones lying on tables.

Dr. Tanaka catches me staring and clears his throat.

"This is my son, Benji. He and his mom just moved from Chicago to join me while I finish my research. Profe said it was okay for him to be here today since my wife had a bunch of job interviews."

Benji nods and gives a small wave. "Hey," he says, picking at a loose thread hanging from the pocket of his khaki shorts.

Maggot nostrils.

A new kid here? That's totally going to distract Arañita. I know this Benji kid will look at me funny as Arañita works hard to arrange the words in my brain correctly so they make sense when I say them. He'll groan when I lose my place in the intake process for the fifth time. And he'll think it's weird that I need a specific kind of black ballpoint pen to write anything because Arañita can't think without it.

Profe nudges me with his elbow, and I realize I've been staring at Benji without saying anything.

"Hi," I mumble as my stomach rolls.

Dr. Tanaka rolls the new cadaver in on a gurney, the metal cart shaking as its wheels clack, and I take a deep breath. I want to show Profe that even though Arañita might bounce between one hundred and thirty-four things in the span of two minutes, I can handle this. I'll just make a point of not looking at Benji.

Dr. Tanaka stops the gurney in front of me as I clench

an iPad in my hands. Pilar Estrada, one of Profe's graduate students, joins us as Dr. Tanaka unzips the thick black body bag containing the person who donated their body to science after they died. Benji gasps and takes a step back behind his dad.

"Welcome to the Dirt Nap Motel," Pilar says to Benji with a smile, tucking a loose strand of her black hair behind her ear. "We still have zero stars on Tripadvisor. Rude."

I look from Profe to the list of things we need to do to process the cadaver before we place it outside in the research field. We use a standard list but I've made sure each item is numbered with a space for me to check it off so I can keep track of what I've done.

My eyes scan the cadaver peeking out from the body bag. It looks like a white man, a little older and paler than my abuelo was when he died. His eyes are closed, like he thought it was a good idea to just take a nap on a cold metal table.

"All right, Frani Fran," Pilar says next to me. Her large tattoo of a skeleton wearing a broad flowered hat moves on her bicep as she ties up her curly hair with a scrunchie. It's by a famous Mexican artist named José Guadalupe Posada. I looked up his drawings online and every single one was of a skeleton wearing regular human clothes. I asked Profe if I could get a tattoo just like Pilar's.

He said no faster than it takes blowflies to start snacking on eyeballs.

Pilar claps, and snaps me from my thoughts. She juts her chin at the cadaver on the table. "Hang on a little bit longer, my buggy friends. You've got a new lunch special headed your way."

She winks at me, and Benji laughs, peeking out a little farther from behind his dad.

"Pilar, let's remember to be respectful," Profe says. Pilar nods and salutes him dramatically.

I shake my head, reading over my list of tasks before Arañita can bounce to thinking about how the last guest we checked into the Dirt Nap Motel was a white woman who had a long scar running down her chest because she'd had a heart transplant. I decided she was probably grateful to the person who donated their heart and wanted to make the most of her life. Arañita was the one who made up a story about the woman running her first marathon, going skydiving, and finally asking out the cute barista at her local coffee shop.

Dr. Tanaka holds out a paper and says, "This is Mr. Rusty Gearhart, age seventy-five. Cause of death is myocardial infarction. He had a heart attack in his sleep. His daughter found him and called an ambulance. The EMTs certified death and brought him here, according to his living will."

"That's really sad," Benji says. His straight black hair

falls across his forehead and he flips it off his face with a sigh.

I look at him and shrug. "It happens."

Mr. Gearhart has a small tattoo in the shape of a heart with the name *Patsy* written in cursive on his shoulder. Arañita pictures Mr. Gearhart pulling up his sleeve and proudly showing Patsy his new tattoo as she gasps and a wide smile spreads across her mouth. Maybe he got it for their thirtieth wedding anniversary and it was his way of telling Patsy he'd love her for at least thirty years more. And then she put on their favorite song, the one that played at their wedding, and they danced barefoot in the middle of their kitchen.

Sometimes Arañita is really sappy.

Profe clears his throat and snaps me from my thoughts. He juts his chin to the iPad in my hands and says, "Why don't you begin, Frani?"

I run my finger along the first item on my list. "Okay," I say, trying my best to sound confident and hold what I'm about to say before Arañita runs past twelve other thoughts. And I don't look at Benji. "Cadaver is a white male, seventy-five years old. The assigned identification number will be 072405."

I triple-check the number I've written down, making sure it shows that this is the fifth donation we've received in July of this year.

Looking at Pilar, I ask her, “Will you please check that livor, algor, and rigor have all happened?”

Pilar groans, rolling her eyes and brushing a stray curl off her forehead with the back of her gloved hand. “You pick me? Ugh. Let’s make the new kid do it.”

Benji’s eyes look like they might pop out of their sockets. “Um, no thank you.”

Pilar is actually an entomologist. Her specialty is studying the bugs that appear on the cadavers we place out in the research field. She has no problem picking up squirming maggots and fat blowflies, but she’s not a big fan of dead bodies and is only working with Profe as part of a special research project she’s doing.

I watch as Pilar takes the cadaver’s temperature, confirming that it’s the same as the temperature in the room.

“Algor, check.”

Next, she tries to lift up the cadaver’s arm. It barely moves, its muscles already frozen in place.

“Rigor, checkity check.”

Finally, she rolls the cadaver slightly to the side so she can see that the skin on his back is a purplish-red color, like a rotten strawberry. This means that his blood has settled to the bottom of his body because of gravity.

“Livor, checkasaurus rex.”

Pilar confirming that the cadaver’s blood has pooled

makes me remember that we need to take a blood sample as part of the process.

"Dr. Tanaka, will you extract a blood sample, please?"

He bites his lip and looks at me with a slight smile. "Are you sure that's what you want me to do next?" he asks.

I check the list on my iPad. We've just completed the second task and drawing samples is way down at number ten. I've messed up. I glance at Benji, expecting to see him rolling his eyes. Instead, he's slowly reaching out a finger to touch Mr. Gearhart's cold skin.

I shake my head. "Oh, right. Uh, next let's take measurements. Dr. Tanaka, will you record his weight, please?"

We step back as Dr. Tanaka guides the gurney over to the large scale we use. While he weighs Mr. Gearhart, I glance at Benji and his *One Piece* T-shirt again. I should ask him if he likes manga as much as I do. But it probably won't matter if we have that in common. Arañita will eventually do something weird enough to make Benji pretend he doesn't even know me.

I'm used to that.

"Did you get it, Frani Fran?" I hear Pilar ask. She nudges me gently with her elbow and I catch myself staring at her tattoo.

Maggot nostrils. Arañita got me distracted again.

"Right, sorry. Could you repeat that?"

My palms sweat and stick to the iPad.

"No worries, he said it really fast. You're just like me. I can never understand things if people talk too fast," Pilar tells me with a wink. She doesn't have to do that. I know this is my fault. Arañita jumped around her brainy bouncy house instead of focusing on what Pilar was saying to me.

Pilar tells me the body's height, waist circumference, and foot length again and I type them into the document. Dr. Tanaka pinches the skin on the body's waist, thigh, and chest to measure the body fat with calipers that give him a number for how thick the fold of skin is.

I stare at him and take deep breaths, wishing he'd hurry up and tell me the measurements before I think of something else. He sets the calipers aside and rattles off a few numbers. I type in the body fat numbers on my document and check that off the list.

So far, so good. And Benji hasn't thrown up yet or laughed at me. I look over the list and see several paragraphs with background information about Mr. Gearhart. He would've provided all of this when he filled out the forms to donate his body. I wonder what he was thinking when he completed them. Did he know a twelve-year-old was going to be in charge of his body after he died?

"What's next, Frani?" Dr. Tanaka says, giving me a smile and bringing my brain back to the room.

"Okay," I say. "Now we need blood, hair, and fingernail samples."

I look at Pilar and she groans. "I will literally rock, paper, scissors with anyone not to do that."

Benji chuckles but steps back when I hold out a small vial for the blood sample.

Dr. Tanaka sticks out his hand in a fist and I catch the corner of Profe's mouth tugging up in a smile.

Pilar and Dr. Tanaka face off. "Rock. Paper. Scissors. Shoot."

Dr. Tanaka shakes his head, two fingers extended, as Pilar smiles, her hand in a fist.

"You got lucky," he says.

"Dad, you always lose that game." Benji chuckles.

Once Dr. Tanaka finishes cutting a chunk of Mr. Gearhart's wispy white hair, the samples are placed in either small bags or vials and tagged with the number I assigned. Profe looks at me from behind his thick glasses. "What's next, Frani?"

I run my finger down my checklist and take another deep breath. The sock on my left foot has slipped down under my heel and all Arañita can think about are the fabric wrinkles pressing into my skin instead of the list in front of me.

Rolling my ankle, I stutter. I think I forgot to check off

something on the list. As I look back over it, I don't have a mark next to photographs, but we should've already done that since we just took samples.

"Did, uh, did we take the pictures we needed?"

Dr. Tanaka nods. "Yep. Whole body, face, teeth, arms, and legs. We did that right after we took measurements."

I bite my lip. That was when I was reading over Mr. Gearhart's background information on the form. There was a list of all the jobs he had during his life, how much money he usually made each year, everywhere he'd ever lived, and whether he smoked or used drugs. I never understood why we needed all that information about a cadaver. It didn't seem to have anything to do with how long it took a person's hair to slide off into the dirt or their skin to turn gray and bloat. But Dr. Tanaka explained that a person's life is sometimes written on their body. Like the form says that Mr. Gearhart has several healed bones in both his hands and his right foot.

When I scan the list of jobs he had, it says he was a mechanic. Maybe he had accidents while he was working. Or maybe he was clumsy. Or maybe a thousand-pound bear barged into his shop and threw a small car on his foot.

"Frani?" Profe clears his throat and raises an eyebrow.

I shake my head and glance at Benji. I can feel my heartbeat in my ears. This is a disaster. Stupid Arañita.

"Um, okay," I say. "I think there's just one thing left.

Tagging the body with its identification number. Right?"

Dr. Tanaka shakes his head. "Mr. Gearhart is part of my study on the effects of different fabrics on the decomposition process, so we need to dress him."

He walks over to a bag on one of the lab tables and pulls out a light purple bundle.

"Oh, that's Mom's favorite sweatshirt. She's gonna be so mad at you," Benji says, smirking at his dad.

I swallow a chuckle as Profe and Dr. Tanaka put the purple sweatshirt along with a matching pair of purple sweatpants on Mr. Gearhart. They have a tough time since all of Mr. Gearhart's limbs are frozen in place.

Then Pilar grabs four tags and writes 072405 on each along with the cadaver's name. I hand two of them to Benji and point to Mr. Gearhart's feet. Even though his hands shake, he loops a tag around each of Mr. Gearhart's big toes while I slip them around each of his wrists. I'm impressed he didn't roll his eyes and tell me I was ridiculous to expect him to do that.

Once we finish, Profe zips up the thick black body bag. Dr. Tanaka pushes the gurney to the main lab door, and we follow him. Profe pats me on the back and says, "You did fine, Frani. Just fine."

I loosen the death grip I had on the iPad. "Thanks," I mumble. I know I didn't do the best. It took us longer to process this body than the others we've done before because

I kept losing my place, daydreaming, and getting distracted.

But Benji didn't once laugh at me or groan. He didn't sigh loudly while I daydreamed and forgot where I was in the intake process.

I wonder how long it'll take for Arañita to mess that up.

THREE

"IS THIS WHERE all the bodies are?" Benji asks as we bounce in the cab of Profe's truck while it goes over limestone rocks weathered by the Texas sun. He stares out the window and his eyes grow wide every time we pass a cadaver.

"Pretty much," I say. I always like riding in Profe's truck. You don't have to look people in the eye when you talk to them. Arañita is always bad at that.

"So this place is called the Forensic Anthropology Research Facility?" Benji bites his lip, thinking. "That makes the acronym FARF. Wouldn't it be better to call it Forensic Anthropology Research and Testing?"

"FART?" I snort as Profe shakes his head and laughs. "There's already enough smells here to keep people away. I don't think we need to go announcing it."

"I guess." Benji shrugs, tapping his foot on the floor of the cab.

I hold on to the hope that Benji is just as weird as I am.

The truck bounces over a large rock and I peek through

the back window to Dr. Tanaka and Pilar grabbing on to the sides of the bed as they make sure the body bag doesn't slide around. Dr. Tanaka gives me a thumbs-up and smiles as Pilar raises her arms in the air like she's on a roller coaster.

Looking over the land stretched in front of us as Profe drives, I spot Ms. Prado, a body we placed in the field two months ago. She's lying on top of the dirt, a wire cage over her because Profe wanted to track her decomposition without coyotes or buzzards interfering. Her body is wrapped in a light pink bathrobe because Dr. Tanaka wanted to test how linen affects decomposition. I squint and can just make out Ms. Prado's white kneecap peeking from the skin that has already faded away into the dirt.

Most people would think this is gross. My fourth-grade teacher asked me to write a different "What I Did Last Summer" essay after I turned in four pages about going with Profe to visit the first body farm established in the United States at the University of Tennessee. Apparently, I was too descriptive with what happens to bodies when they lie out in the sun, wind, and rain.

I turned in one short paragraph about getting free Whataburger from Essie instead.

Boring.

"I think it's about time to bring that one in," Profe says, pointing to a cadaver that's entirely bone lying under the low branch of a live oak tree. Someone wandering past might think it's just a pile of rocks, but no one just walks by the body farm. We have a tall fence to keep people out and a security gate at the entrance that requires a special code. And on top of that, the body farm sits in the middle of 3,500 acres run by the university's agriculture department, filled with cows, sheep, and goats. No one is going to just happen upon this place.

It also makes it difficult to invite friends over.

But that's not really an issue for me.

"All right, here we go," Profe says as he brings the truck to a stop next to a patch of prickly pear cactus.

Benji and I hop out and help Dr. Tanaka and Pilar place the body bag on the ground. The thick black fabric is already hot from the blazing Texas summer sun. Dr. Tanaka and Profe unzip the body bag, slip on gloves, and place Mr. Gearhart's body gently on the ground.

"Frani Fran, did you make sure we took a body fat measurement? I don't remember doing that," Pilar asks, tightening the scrunchie in her hair.

Arañita starts flying around her web, trying to remember each step of the intake process I completed. But I can't picture myself taking that particular measurement. Clenching my fists in frustration, I walk over to Profe and ask to see his iPad. Out of the corner of my eye, I see Pilar take something out of her pocket and crouch next to Mr. Gearhart's head.

Once Profe scrolls through the intake list on the iPad and we see that I did actually get the body fat measurement, Dr. Tanaka pulls a wire cage from the bed of the truck and sets it over the body. This will let in any bugs that help with decomposition but keep out any larger animals that might want to drag Mr. Gearhart somewhere else on the property.

Profe grabs a hammer and places a wooden stake in the ground with a metal tag attached that has all the identifying information for the body. Finally, I take the iPad and drop a location pin on a map so Mr. Gearhart's final resting place is marked with GPS.

Dr. Tanaka removes his gloves and pats me on the back. "Nice job today, Frani."

Pilar nods. "I think he'd rate you a ten out of ten for the Dirt Nap Motel," she says, pointing to Mr. Gearhart.

"This was actually pretty cool," Benji says with a small smile.

Profe gives me a thumbs-up. Maybe things didn't go as badly as I thought.

"Okay, team, let's collect some bones and then we'll head in," Profe says.

Once a cadaver has lost all its organs, muscle, and tissue, Profe takes the skeleton to his lab on campus, where it'll get cleaned up and used to teach students how to identify different bones. I like to sit in the lab and test myself to see if I can tell a shin bone from a forearm bone or the hip bone of a male skeleton from a female skeleton.

"Frani, what do you think?" Profe asks.

I shake my head. I totally missed what he said. "About what?"

"Are you going to help us collect the skeleton?"

Arañita wore out my brain. Today has already been a lot: trying to focus on the steps of the intake, making sure Benji doesn't think I'm two steps away from ultimate weirdness, having to concentrate as Dr. Tanaka and Pilar talk.

I bite my lip. "Pass. I think I'll walk around instead."

Profe nods and heads to the truck.

Benji hangs back. "Do you think I could stay with you? I've hit my limit for touching dead bodies."

Arañita tells me that Benji hanging around just means more opportunities for me to do something strange. He'll probably run up the hill, trip over a dead body, and never want to talk to me again.

But instead I say, "Sure."

After Dr. Tanaka makes Benji promise he won't tell his mom he walked around the body farm unsupervised, Profe, Dr. Tanaka, and Pilar drive away. Benji and I meander around a patch of cacti, down the hill a little, and to a large rock set in the middle of a field filled with tall grass. I can barely make out the wooden stake and metal flag next to the rock, but I know it's there.

"This is Winston," I say, sitting down on the rock and

looking at the skeleton lying in the dirt next to it. His bones have been bleached white by the sun, the jawbone detached from the skull, the whole skeleton lying flat on the ground like something ran over it. That's what happens to a body after so many years in the Texas sun and heat. Profe normally would've brought this skeleton to the lab a while ago. Maybe he's tracking something with it that takes longer.

"Wow," Benji says, sitting down next to me. "How long has that one been here?"

"Over ten years. Profe told me that when Winston came to the body farm, he had a huge right calf muscle. His left arm was darker than his right and completely covered with freckles and moles. Profe said that showed Winston had been a truck driver his entire life."

"Huh," Benji says, scanning Winston as he bites a nail.

Without thinking, Arañita pushes a word flood out of my mouth before I can stop her. "I wrote a story yesterday about the cadaver that Profe placed out here last week. When I was helping with the body processing, Profe pointed out that the cadaver had really high bone density. Like, her bones were super thick! I looked at the cadaver's personal information and saw she was a bodybuilder. Your dad explained weight lifting increases bone density.

"So in my story, Ms. Soto, the cadaver, saves the day when she lifts a school bus off a motorcyclist that crashed into it. Then she tosses the burning motorcycle into a nearby swimming pool like it's a Frisbee. Everyone watching cheers her on and the kids she saved take turns dangling from her flexed biceps. I uploaded it to Story Stack and it only got a couple of comments. But that's okay."

I pick at the end of my shoelace and catch my breath. I look at Benji, but he's still chewing on his nail.

Maggot nostrils. Arañita's done it. Once she lands on a thread she loves, she plucks at it until I'm completely out of words. My babbling makes eyes glaze over at school in record time. Benji will never talk to me again after that info dump. He's going to beg his dad to never make him come to the body farm again to hang out with the girl who writes stories about dead bodies.

A red-tailed hawk flies from the pecan tree behind us and lands on a metal cage farther into the field. It pokes its beak between the wires but can't get at the body lying on the ground. Giving up, it flies away toward the fence.

"That sounds awesome," Benji finally says.

My mouth drops open. "Really?"

He smiles. "Well, yeah. I love reading action stories. But my favorite are horror stories. Have you ever read *Dissolving Classroom* by Junji Ito?"

I think I might pass out on the ground right next to Winston.

"Are you kidding? He's my favorite. That's such a strange story. I love the illustrations. You can always tell a Junji Ito drawing," I say, practically breathless. I clench my fists to keep from talking even though Arañita wants me to list my top ten horror manga ever and tell him about *Ghost Book* by Remy Lai, which I just read.

Benji smiles. "I thought this summer was going to be boring. Mom and I had to wait until our house sold in Chicago before we could come down here with Dad. I figured I'd be stuck at home all day because I didn't know anyone. But this is really cool. More dead people than I'm used to, but still cool."

I hop up from the rock we're sitting on and step around Winston. "Do you want see the cattle that are on the agricultural ranch?" I ask. "They pick their noses with their tongues."

Arañita, why are you trying to mess this up?

"Are they alive? Like they're not decomposing cows or skeleton bulls?" Benji says, brushing his hands on his shorts.

I laugh. "They're totally alive. I promise."

We walk down the hill to the fence that separates the body farm from the agricultural ranch. I stare through the wire fence at a large Black Angus cow chewing on grass, her jaw rolling around as her tail flicks insects away.

Something brushes against my leg, probably a winding branch of the mesquite bush I'm standing next to, and I slap it away absentmindedly with my fingers. It scratches me again and I shake my leg. But something holds on to the fabric of my pants.

I look down.

That's when I see it.

A hand shoots from behind a rock and wraps around my ankle.

FOUR

FINGERS GRIP MY ankle tightly as jagged nails press into my skin.

"What is that?" Benji shouts, jumping back.

I scream and shake my leg as the hand writhes in the dirt, revealing an arm emerging from between two rocks. Benji rushes over, trying to help me push back at the fingers digging into my skin.

Kicking hard enough to free myself, I run from the fence and the hand clawing the air at the loss of its victim. Benji races behind me, still mumbling "What was that?" over and over. I turn back just in time to see another arm push a rock aside and grip the wires of the fence for leverage.

The muscles in my legs burn as I scramble up the rocks and across patches of grass. Benji and I are completely out of breath as we run up the hill toward my house, wanting to put as much distance between us and whatever just popped up out of the ground. The hot sun beats down on my back as we race past Mr. Gearhart and the buzzards circling the metal cage we put over him.

When Benji and I finally reach the long porch that borders the back of my house, I collapse on the steps. Wiping away the hair that's stuck to my cheeks with sweat, I squeeze my eyes closed, trying to erase the image of the bony fingers wrapped around my ankle.

There's no way that happened. It's impossible.

I'm hallucinating from heat exhaustion. Texas gets ridiculously hot in the summer. I fried some brain cells working outside with Profe, Dr. Tanaka, and Pilar. That's why I imagined something pushing through the rocks.

"Does that usually happen?" Benji asks, still struggling to catch his breath as he sits on the steps next to me.

Okay . . . so Benji saw it too. Which means it was all real.

Maggot nostrils.

For the rest of the day, I try to distract myself. That's usually not a difficult task. Give Arañita two seconds of free time and she'll be off, swinging from web to web, without a destination.

But today, Arañita always comes back around to the same silky thread—fingers creeping across the ground, reaching for me.

Benji and I sat in silence on my porch steps before he finally mumbled, "I think I'd better find my dad and go home."

He's probably never coming back to the body farm. He definitely thinks I'm a weird girl who lives in an even weirder place.

As Profe and I sit at dinner, eating the slightly burnt grilled cheeses he made, I don't dare tell him what happened. He's always worried about when he's going to get a call from one of my teachers because I blurted something out in class I shouldn't have, when Essie and I are going to yell at each other like howler monkeys, or that I lost my cell phone for the twelfth time. I don't need to add to his worries about me. I don't know how I'd explain what happened anyway. The only reason I know it wasn't completely my imagination is that Benji saw it too.

I bite into my grilled cheese and butter runs down my chin. Before I can stop her, Arañita takes over and I blurt out, "Has anything ever come back to life on the body farm?"

Profe's eyes widen as a string of cheese dangles from his mouth. "I love your stories, Frani, but I think you know that's not scientifically possible."

I should shut up, but Arañita pushes the words out of my mouth. "People come back to life all the time, don't they? Like their hearts get shocked back by those machines—"

"Defibrillators?"

"Yeah, those," I say, gesturing with a triangle slice of grilled cheese. "And there are lots of instances of people coming back to life in the hospital after the doctors said they were dead, right?"

Profe takes a long sip of Dr Pepper. "Do you know that for a fact or have you just seen it in movies?"

"Okay, fine. Probably just in movies. But it's got to be possible, right? There are so many things that could happen. Maybe we just thought a body was dead and they woke up when we placed them out in the field. Maybe they were in a coma and the shock of being poked by a bunch of scientists who then set them in the middle of nowhere so bugs could crawl all over them snapped them back to life."

I know I'm just thinking out loud right now. I can't stop myself. At least Profe is used to this and listens as I ramble. Once it's obvious I've finished my word flood, he takes a deep breath.

"Let's look at it scientifically," he says, folding his paper napkin into a tight triangle. "We make sure that all cadavers exhibit livor, algor, and rigor mortis—"

"I know."

Profe holds up a finger. It's always hard for Arañita to not interrupt.

"It's not only those things that indicate a person is clinically dead. Did you know it's not a heartbeat that determines life or death? It's brain activity. And all bodies received at the facility show no brain activity. And there's no way to bring brain activity back once it's lost. You can't jump-start a brain like you can a heart."

"Or a car."

Profe nods. "And consider this too—decomposition begins immediately after death and only increases once we place a cadaver out in the field. All manner of maggots and blowflies begin to feed on the body."

"And they lay lots of eggs in the nose, mouth, and lots of other places, right?" I ask.

Profe opens his mouth to answer but we hear a groan behind us.

Essie stands at the end of the hallway, an empty plate in her hand.

"This is why I eat in my room instead of with you two," she says, rolling her eyes.

Profe chuckles and flicks his napkin triangle at me before looking at the both of us. "Remember I'll be at a conference in San Antonio tomorrow and won't be able to answer any calls. Frani, if you need anything, call Essie, and Essie, don't forget to keep you phone near."

"So *I'm* responsible for her? Again?" Essie mumbles. She starts to put her plate in the dishwasher, but instead slams it shut and narrows her eyes. I squirm in my seat. This won't be good.

"Frani, you forgot to unload the dishwasher again. I've reminded you for the past six days. We're seriously running out of clean plates," she says. She flips her hair and marches down the hall, calling over her shoulder, "Get it done!"

I didn't forget. Every time I put a dirty cup in the sink, I know I need to do the dishes. But Arañita acts completely overwhelmed by the steps required to unload the dishwasher and put everything where it belongs. So instead, she just whispers, "Tomorrow. Just do it tomorrow."

And then tomorrow, she still feels the same way. And I'm left eating cereal out of an empty plastic butter container.

Now that I can't stop thinking about whatever grabbed me out in the field, there's no way I'll be able to focus on dishes.

That evening, as I lie in bed, still trying to calm down, I look at my ankle again. The red mark is gone, faded after I scrubbed it practically raw in the hottest shower I've ever taken and slathered it with Essie's most expensive body lotion that she will most likely yell at me about later.

My phone buzzes and I jump. No one ever texts me.

Hey it's Benji. My dad asked your dad for your number. Is it okay to text you?

My heart jumps in my throat. He still wants to talk to me? Even after all the body farm weirdness on top of my usual weirdness today?

With shaking fingers, I text him back. It's okay. Thanks for asking. Have you . . . recovered from today?

I watch three dots blink over and over on my phone. Benji's probably thinking of a nice way to tell me that he won't ever come back to the body farm.

My phone buzzes.

Had to change my shorts but yeah. So can I come back tomorrow? My dad said it was okay.

My eyebrows rise and I read his text again three times to check what Benji is saying.

You actually want to come back? Even with what happened? I'm sorry I got distracted a lot and said weird things.

A scratching sound at my window distracts me as I wait for Benji to respond. It's light and I can only hear it if I concentrate. But where is it coming from? There aren't any trees next to my window whose branches could reach the glass.

Wait, you think YOU'RE the weird thing that happened? Not the dead hand shooting out of the rocks and grabbing you? I gotta be honest and say I think your priorities might be a little off.

I shake my head. Maybe I'm focusing on Arañita and her web so I don't think about whatever grabbed me in the field? I shiver.

Yeah, that's definitely it.

Okay so we both agree that something grabbed me. But it couldn't be one of the cadavers. It's not scientifically possible.

My brain bounces back to my conversation with Profe. There's no way a body that was alive could make it through the body farm's intake process. And there's no way that a body that passed all the benchmarks for being dead could suddenly come back to life.

My phone buzzes as another message from Benji pops up.

Well, if science says it's not possible, what's the explanation?

Arañita slams six separate thoughts into my brain, and I wince as I try to sort through them. The best I can text Benji back is, I don't know. But both our parents are scientists. They probably wouldn't believe us and then we'd be in trouble all summer for making up a story.

Before I set my phone on my nightstand, it buzzes one more time.

I'll help you figure it out tomorrow.

I wrap my comforter around my shoulders and grab my iPad. Opening to a blank document, I start typing a story about Mr. Gearhart to distract myself from the noise outside, the soreness in my ankle, and the images of a hand shooting up out of the ground.

My fingers fly across my keyboard as I imagine Mr. Gearhart working on the engine of a car to make it speed faster than an airplane. Arañita calms down as I write, as if my story grabs her attention and doesn't let her think about twelve random things like she normally does.

Once I realized that typing made Arañita a lot happier

than using a pen or pencil, I liked writing a whole lot more. Arañita would always get frustrated with me because I couldn't move my hand as fast as she was coming up with the story. And forget being able to read my handwriting. It looks like ink-covered maggots squirming across the page.

The scratching outside fades as my story continues and Mr. Gearhart surprises Patsy with a cross-country road trip for their fortieth anniversary in a light blue Mustang he rebuilt. My eyelids grow heavy and my typing slows down as Mr. Gearhart teaches his granddaughter how to check the oil in her car and inflate the tires.

I save my story and set my iPad on my nightstand. Wrapping myself in my comforter, the pressure of the fabric relaxes my muscles and slows my breathing. I drift into sleep but my dreams are still preoccupied with the events of the day—the stress of being in charge of Mr. Gearhart's intake quickly followed by the surprise out in the field.

I can't tell if it's part of my dream, the breeze outside, or something else, but a scratchy voice slips into my ear, whispering over and over.

"Help . . . me."

FIVE

"I NEVER EXPECTED there to be so much . . . liquid," Benji says, kicking his foot in the dirt as we stand over Cadaver 072201 in the field. Profe placed the body under a cage next to a live oak tree last week and the hot Texas summer means it's in the bloat stage.

In fifth grade, I not-so-accidentally described what happens to a cadaver during the bloat stage in the middle of the San Zavala Elementary cafeteria because Arañita kept plucking that string. My description of gases building up in a body and puffing out the skin earned me a trip to the school counselor. I guess spaghetti day was ruined forever.

"So where should we start?" Benji asks.

I point down the hill. "Maybe over by the fence. That's where it happened."

I lead Benji toward the fence, passing Winston and Cadaver 032306, whose left shoulder is being pecked at by a curious crow. Benji swallows hard.

"You're really used to this stuff, aren't you?" he asks.

I shrug. "It's just science."

"I'm pretty sure I never covered anything like this in science class. When Dad started studying all this stuff, my mom wouldn't let me look at any of his textbooks or research. She said it wasn't appropriate."

I smirk and point at the *Death Note* T-shirt Benji is wearing. "You're wearing a shirt from a manga about writing people's names in a notebook so they die. Your mom has strange ideas about what's appropriate."

Benji nods as I stop in front of Cadaver 082305 and crouch down. Its eyes, nose, and mouth are completely covered with small yellowish maggots squirming across its sagging skin.

"Listen," I tell Benji.

He stands behind me, not wanting to get closer to the body, but leans forward a little.

"Do you hear it? The popping noise?" I ask him, raising my eyebrow.

"Yeah. What is that?" he says, his voice shaking slightly.

I chuckle. "It's the Rice Krispies effect. That's what maggots sound like when they're feeding on a body."

Benji groans and takes a step back. "Oh geez, Frani. You just ruined my favorite snack. Like forever."

"It's not that bad, right?" I smile nervously. Did Arañita do something too weird again? "The way I see it, these people all decided to donate their bodies so they could help scientists help other people. I think that's cool."

"Maybe," Benji says. "But I'm still never eating Rice Krispies Treats again."

The smile on his face makes me feel better. Like maybe he's okay with all the strange stuff that Arañita tumbles out of my mouth. The kids at school aren't like this. When I was in third grade, I got invited over to Clarissa Morgan's house for a spa day birthday party. Her mom tried to put pink fake nails on my fingers, but I told her that I couldn't wear them under gloves while I was examining dead bodies. The nail length bothered Arañita too much anyway.

I didn't get invited to any birthday parties after that.

Once Benji and I get to the fence between the body farm and the agricultural field, he points to a mound of dirt.

"This is where it happened, right?" he asks, picking up a twig and pushing the dirt and rocks around.

I nod. "Yeah. I was standing here while we were staring at that random cow and all of a sudden, I felt something grab my leg. When I looked down, there was this hand wrapped around my ankle."

Benji keeps pushing dirt around. "Something big came out of here. These rocks have all been pushed aside."

I run my fingers along the fence. "And look here. The fence is pulled up from the dirt. Like something pushed its way through from the other side."

"Maybe a coyote? Dad tells me those are everywhere," Benji says.

I shake my head. "The hand that grabbed me was definitely . . . human."

"So do you really think it was one of the bodies that's out here? From what I've seen so far, none of them seem like they could do something like that. They're all too busy being maggot food."

Benji tosses his stick aside and stands.

I sigh and lift my foot to look at the red mark on my ankle again. Arañita bounces all over the place and I can hardly string three words together. I squint at the loose rocks next to the fence and see a mound of maggots pulsing in the ground. A swarm of blowflies buzz around the hole, searching for something that's no longer there.

Arañita finally lands on a thought, something I can hardly believe is true, and I open my mouth to tell Benji.

That's when I hear the growl.

Benji and I spin around and spot a person standing under the tall live oak tree next to Cadaver 102108. Shoulders heaving, the person growls again.

Benji and I jump back, and I grab his hand.

"You're . . . you're not supposed to be here," I say, my breath catching in my throat.

The person is wearing a dirty red hoodie over their head. Their hands shake at their sides as they take a shuffling step forward, dust swirling around their feet.

They open their mouth and a wheezing sound floats down the hill toward me and Benji.

I narrow my eyes and examine the person. It's the only way to distract myself from the fact that I can feel my heartbeat in my toes, making Arañita swing furiously from thread to thread.

Underneath their hoodie, the person has reddish skin around their mouth, nose, and eyes. They hold out their hand and a clump of maggots falls to the ground from their sleeve.

"Frani, who is that?" Benji asks by my side, squeezing my hand and pulling me from my thoughts.

The person takes another step toward us, kicking up dirt as their foot drags. Their mouth opens again, their lips cracked and their tongue swollen.

"Help . . . me."

I swallow hard and push Benji behind me. I recognize that sound, that voice. That's what I heard last night as I was trying to go to sleep. I squeeze my eyes shut, trying to make Arañita calm down long enough so I can put together all the information she's bouncing between.

The loose rocks with maggots, the blowflies in the air, the reddish skin on the person's face, their swollen tongue and filthy clothes.

"Help me," they say again, their body shuddering as their chest heaves.

I shake my head and clear my throat, trying to get my words in the right order.

"I've got bad news for you," I finally blurt out. "You're dead."

SIX

"NOPE NOPE NOPE," Benji mumbles, shaking his head and stepping farther away from the person still shuffling toward us.

I narrow my eyes and take a cautious step forward, closer to the person's outstretched hand. Arañita can't help but examine them. They're just a little bit taller than I am and there's a purplish bruise on their wrist surrounding a black wound, like something was eating away at their skin. The nail of their index finger is gone and I watch a beetle crawl from under the sleeve of their hoodie, skitter down their pants, and across the ground.

"I'm . . . what?" the person says, lowering their arm and stumbling toward the rock I usually sit on when I talk to Winston.

I clear my throat and wave my hand in front of my face, shooing away the blowflies that circle the person. They look like half the guys Essie goes to school with, except for the bugs and rotting skin, which makes me think they're probably just a few years older than I am.

"I'm pretty sure you're dead," I say. "You're kind of checking a lot of boxes for not being among the living anymore."

The person squeezes their eyes shut, their eyelids briefly sticking together when they try to open them again. They bite their lip and their teeth go straight through their skin. But no blood pools on their lips.

"Not . . . possible," they mumble.

Benji takes a tentative step closer to me. "I'm gonna agree with the horror movie main character here. How is that even possible?"

The person's torso heaves and they fall onto the rock next to Winston. They rest their hands on their knees and take several ragged breaths, ending in a cough that wracks their chest.

I move closer to the person. "It's obviously difficult for you to move. That's possible rigor mortis."

I place a hand on my forehead and a hand on the person's forehead. Benji gasps. The person's skin feels loose, as if any moment it might slide off their face.

"Your body temperature is the same as the environment, at least from what I can tell by touching your skin. That's algor mortis. And the way you bit your lip but no blood came out means it's probably pooled at the back of your body. That's livor mortis."

Arañita forgets that I'm standing next to a potentially reanimated dead body. I reach out and hold the person's wrist. They don't even react to my touch, their muscles looking like they might melt into the rock at any moment.

"Frani, what the heck are you doing?" Benji asks.

"This is definitely an injury," I say, holding up the person's wrist and pointing to the wound just under their palm. A web of black veins spread from the center of the bruise. "I can't quite tell what it's from. Maybe a spider or snakebite. Maybe from the barbed wire fence."

I let go of the person's arm and it takes a few moments for them to lower their arm back to rest on their leg.

"Do you know how you got here? How did you get hurt?" I ask. Those are just the first two of the thirty-seven questions Arañita tries to ask them.

"How did you come back to life and grab Frani?" Benji adds.

The person finally looks up and meets my gaze. The whites of their eyes have a yellow hue. I notice that their pupils don't get smaller when they look into the bright sun behind me and add that to my "this person is definitely dead" list.

They lick their lips, their swollen tongue looking more like a slug than a human body part. Their eyes search my face, as if the answer is written in my frizzy hair or the pimples that wander across my chin.

"I . . . don't know. Can't . . . remember," they wheeze.

I cross my arms and purse my lips. "Well, regardless, you're obviously dead."

Benji pushes me gently in the shoulder. "Kind of a harsh way to give somebody bad news, don't you think?"

Arañita has always had a problem with being too straightforward and honest. It takes too much effort for me to arrange the words Arañita is throwing out of my mouth for me to make sure they fit what people call "polite" or "gentle."

"What am I supposed to say? We could dance around the facts all day and still land in the same place. This person is dead. I don't know how they came back to life, but it's a fact. There's no other way around it."

Benji opens his mouth to protest but a growl fills the air. The person stands up from the rock, their face contorting in pain as their muscles stretch. They stumble toward us, gasping for air. A blood vessel bursts in their left eye, flooding the yellowish shade with bright red.

"No," they seethe. "No!"

They can't stop their momentum as they knock me over and stumble down the hill. I fall hard in the dirt, rocks digging into the backs of my legs and my palms. Benji helps me up and when we stare after the person, they've already disappeared into the mesquite bushes at the bottom of the hill.

"Are you okay?" Benji asks, picking a leaf out of my hair.

"I think so. I'm all right."

"From the fall or the encounter with a potential zom—Nope, can't say it."

I take a deep breath. "From meeting a possibly reanimated corpse?"

Benji shrugs. "That's a mouthful, but better than the Z-word."

We walk down the hill toward the mesquite bushes, but there's no sign of the person.

"Well, now what?" Benji asks, kicking the dirt with his shoe.

"We can't just let them wander around. We have to find them," I say, putting my hands on my hips. "What if someone thinks Profe can't run the body farm properly? And then they'll pull his funding and we'll have to move. And what if I have to start all over at a new school?"

Benji raises an eyebrow. "Okay, maybe before we spiral down into a bottomless pit of doom, we should just try to find the PUD?"

I raise my eyebrow. "PUD?"

"Potentially Undead Dude. Anything to keep from saying the Z-word."

I smirk. "Okay, fine. We have to go find the PUD. If they wander onto campus, that could be a disaster. They could lose an arm in the middle of the quad, snack on unsuspecting freshmen in the student center. Oh god, what if they make a whole army of the undead from the football team?"

Benji puts his hand on my shoulder. "Take a breath, Frani."

Arañita barely listens to him and keeps jumping around to all the horrible things that might happen.

"We'll figure this out. This PUD is just a boss-level challenge," Benji reassures me.

We head across the field toward the far gate that leads through the agricultural center and on to campus, and I glance at Benji as he stares at a longhorn cow chewing on a clump of grass. "You're really okay with all of this? It's not too much?" I ask.

Benji shrugs. "I figure I could either be at home unpacking boxes with my mom and doing her endless lists of chores or out here chasing after dead people. I'm as surprised as you that the second one is the better option."

We march through the agricultural center, looking for any sign of the PUD—a half-eaten cow, a leg lying in the dirt, an undead coyote crawling across the ground.

But there's nothing.

"How can we even be sure they came this way?" Benji asks.

"They were asking for help, right? I think they'd probably try to go to a place with more people. That way they could find someone to help them. Which is exactly what we need to keep them from doing."

Benji looks at me as we walk and purses his lips.

"I'm sorry," I say before he can respond. "That probably didn't make any sense."

Smiling, Benji nudges me with his elbow. "Don't worry. It did."

When we finally arrive on campus, it's bustling with students shuffling from building to building. A group of students kick around a soccer ball on a patch of grass, and a few others are flying a drone over some trees. Luckily, because it's summer, there aren't as many students as there will be in a couple of weeks when everyone comes back to campus for the fall semester.

"How are we going to find the PUD among all these people?" Benji asks.

I shrug. "I guess look for somebody in a red hoodie?"

Benji groans and waves his hand at a crowd of students pouring out of the student center. "Half of these people are wearing red."

I sigh, remembering that Central Texas University's school colors are red and gray. Most of the students on campus are wearing some sort of red shirt or tank top. Finding our PUD is going to be more difficult than we thought.

When Benji and I wander past the towering library, a voice calls after us.

"What are you doing here?"

I turn and see Essie standing on the steps of the library,

three thick books in her arms.

Shoving my hands into the pockets of my shorts, I bite my lip. Arañita comes up with seven things to tell Essie, but I can't bring myself to say any of them because there's no way she would believe me.

Essie waves her hand in front of my face as I stare at the books in her arms, immediately distracted by the titles.

"Hello? I asked you a question," she says.

I grunt and cross my arms. Essie never lets Arañita take a moment to gather her thoughts. She doesn't understand that I even *have* an Arañita. Lately, it seems like all she does is try to control me, so we don't have another Disaster Day.

"We're searching for a Potentially Undead Dude that might be wandering around campus," Benji says with a completely straight face.

Essie looks him up and down and rolls her eyes. "And you are?"

"This is Benji. He's Dr. Tanaka's son. I'm showing him around campus." I turn to Benji and jut my thumb toward Essie. "This is my sister."

Essie purses her lips. "Sure, whatever. Not like you could pay attention long enough to find anything. And this campus isn't a playground. Don't be annoying."

As Essie stomps away from us, Benji calls after her, "But being annoying is my specialty!"

When Essie is out of sight, Arañita finally thinks of five

comebacks to shout after her. Arañita's timing is officially the worst.

"Why'd you tell her we were looking for a PUD?" I ask as we continue our search past the student union and the bronze Juneteenth statue in front of the history building.

Benji shrugs. "I felt like she wasn't going to believe anything we told her. So might as well dazzle her with the truth."

I chuckle as we round the football stadium, much bigger than it should be for a university this size, but this is Texas. With still no sign of our PUD, we walk along the riverbank that winds through the middle of campus where students like to lie out between classes . . . or instead of going to classes. We're just about to give up as we trudge along the promenade lined with classroom buildings when I spot a red hoodie in the distance.

"There," I say, pointing to a figure turned away from us, sitting on a bench in front of the math building.

"Is that the PUD?" Benji asks as we approach.

The person's hoodie doesn't look like those of the rest of the students we've seen. It's got thick dirt smudges on it and the hem is completely frayed.

As we draw closer, I hear heavy breathing. I reach my hand out to touch the PUD's shoulder, but Benji stops me.

"Wait. Listen," he whispers.

The PUD's heavy breathing is broken up by heaving shoulders. A gurgling sound rises from their throat.

They're crying.

I walk around to face the PUD. They look up and the skin around their eyes is red but there are no tears streaming down their cheeks. I wouldn't expect any.

"Are you okay?" I ask, talking a small step toward the PUD.

They hold out a hand to me and Benji gasps. Lying in the center of their palm is a single finger. I glance at their other hand and notice their pinky missing.

"You . . . were . . . right."

SEVEN

WALKING BACK ACROSS campus with a PUD should be risky business. But most students are busy looking at their phones, furiously reading textbooks right before a test, or running to classes they're late for because they overslept.

No one seems to notice two kids and a slow-moving person heading toward the agricultural center. We walk at a snail's pace since the PUD shuffles and groans with each step. Benji eyes the person warily when we pass a group of cows munching on prairie grass.

"You're not feeling hungry, are you?" he asks.

I raise my eyebrow at him, and he shrugs. The PUD doesn't answer, their gaze fixed ahead. We convinced them to come back with us to Profe's lab. There's so much to figure out—who they are, how they died, how they came back to life. And how to fix the whole situation of something being alive that probably shouldn't be. Arañita can hardly be still as we walk, and I bite my lip and clench my fists to keep from blurting out everything I'm thinking to Benji and the PUD.

As we pass through the gate between the agricultural center and the body farm, Benji points to the PUD shuffling in front of us and asks, "Shouldn't we tell our dads about . . . this? I know we thought they wouldn't believe us about the hand popping out of the rocks, but the body attached to that hand is wandering around now."

I squeeze my eyes open and closed, trying to focus my thoughts on his question and not the tangle of other threads Arañita is jumping between. But I can't help clinging to the fact that Benji said "we." I haven't been a part of a "we" for a long time and it's nice to not feel like I'm on my own.

"Maybe. But Profe's speaking in San Antonio at some conference. Your dad is helping him. I think we're on our own for now. So, first things first," I say. "We should figure out who they are. Best way to do that would be to determine when they died."

"You can do that?" Benji asks, stepping widely around Cadaver 052201 as we approach Profe's lab.

"Yeah, there are temperature measurements I can take, and we can also look at the amount of decomposition that's taken place. That'll give us a clue how long they've been dead," I explain.

"But they're not dead anymore," Benji says, raising an eyebrow at the PUD. They don't react to our conversation, shuffling their feet in the dirt with their head lowered. "Don't you think we need to figure out how they went from 'rest in peace' to 'brains brains brains'?"

I start to respond, to tell Benji we're probably dealing with something that has never happened before in science, only in the best movies and TV shows, but when we burst into the lab, I see we're not alone.

"Hey there, Frani Fran!" Pilar shouts, spinning around from the computer she's standing in front of. She looks surprised to see us and raises an eyebrow when she sees the PUD. "Who's your friend?"

Oh, maggot nostrils. I might be able to convince Profe that this PUD came out of the rocks at the body farm, but Pilar will never believe me. Even if I try to, she'd start a long rant about bugs, give us the plot of the telenovela she just watched, and end up sharing a recipe for enchiladas. That would be annoying, but Arañita does the same thing. We need to focus on the PUD now and Pilar will just distract us.

"New student," Benji says quickly, as if reading my mind. "We're giving them a tour."

Pilar looks like she'd be more likely to believe us if we'd just told her we farted out a flock of flying guinea pigs from our butts.

The PUD lowers their head and shoves their hands into the pockets of their hoodie, hiding their missing finger.

"Oh well, enjoy the Dirt Nap Motel. Please give us five

stars," Pilar says, heading around us toward the lab door. "If you're not too tied up with your tour, do you think y'all could help me out in the field for a bit? I'm tracking a specific kind of beetle that feeds off dead tissue and I lost one of my samples."

"You lost a beetle?" I ask, stepping in front of the PUD to block Pilar's view of them.

She tucks two small vials in her jacket pocket and nods. "Um, yeah. I'm usually better at keeping track of things but I can't seem to find this one. You know how that is, Frani."

Unfortunately, I do. Arañita is phenomenal at making sure I misplace things.

"We'd love to help but we have to work on some chores Profe gave us while he's out of town," I say, hoping Pilar doesn't ask exactly what the chores are.

Thankfully, Pilar just nods and opens the lab door. "No worries, Frani Fran," she calls over her shoulder. "Oh, did I tell you about the chilaquiles I made for dinner last night?"

Before Pilar can give us the step-by-step recipe, she heads out of the lab. I lead Benji and the PUD to one of the tables and we shiver at the cold air that blasts through the vents. At least Benji and I do. The PUD stands still next to me, taking it all in.

"We're gonna figure everything out. I promise," I tell them. "We just need to get some information. Do you think I could take your temperature?"

The PUD looks me up and down and licks their lips again with their swollen tongue. I pull a stool out from under the table Benji and I are standing in front of and pat the top. "It's okay."

Taking a deep breath and wincing as their muscles struggle to move, the PUD shuffles over and sits down. I take their temperature and compare it to the temperature outside. It's the same.

"Math time," I say. "A dead body's temperature will decrease one point five degrees every hour until it's the same as the temperature around it. With it being so hot outside right now, the body temperature will likely increase instead of decrease. So we can take their current temperature and the normal body temperature of humans and figure out how many hours it's been since they died."

"I was promised there wouldn't be any math," Benji smirks. He grabs a blank piece of paper and a pencil from a desk in the corner and sits across from the PUD.

I write down the PUD's temperature and they glance at my paper.

"Eight point six . . . degrees," the PUD says.

Benji raises an eyebrow. "Wow. You're quick at math."

"I think so?" The PUD narrows their eyes as if trying to remember.

"That means by the time you grabbed my ankle yesterday, you'd probably been dead for six hours," I say.

Benji eyes the PUD and starts sketching them on the blank paper he has. "Any chance you remember dying?" he asks. "Probably not a great thing to remember, but it would help us."

The PUD grips their hands in their lap and stares at Benji. While they're distracted, I pull back the corner of their red hoodie and reveal their left ear. Part of their hair sticks to the hoodie and pulls off their scalp. A cadaver's hair mat usually falls off after a week or so. This doesn't match with my temperature information. Maybe the PUD being up and walking around is speeding up the decomposition process?

The PUD sighs and slowly taps the side of their head. "Don't . . . remember. Like a clogged garbage disposal . . . up here."

A mass of maggots squirms and falls out of their ear. Benji covers his mouth, squeezing his eyes shut. I take a vial and collect the maggots with some tweezers. "We can count the number of maggots to get information about how long the PUD was in the ground too."

Benji swallows hard and leans away from me. "I'll leave that job to you."

I search the shelves in the lab. "I know Pilar has a chart somewhere about this since bugs are her thing. It shows how many maggots are usually on a cadaver each hour after death."

Benji continues drawing the PUD—the outline of their face, the sagging skin on their cheeks, their sunken eyes. The PUD just sits there, their eyes slowly moving from Benji to me and back again. They tap their index and ring finger on the leg of their jeans over and over.

"You know," Benji says, "you seem to talk about getting distracted all the time. But you're not getting distracted now. What's the difference?"

I chuckle as I find Pilar's notebook. I flip through it, scanning equations, drawings of beetles and cadavers, and charts filled with numbers. Several pages in the middle are ripped out. I hope that wasn't the information we needed.

"I could do this all day!" I answer Benji. "Stuff at school is usually boring. Ara—I mean, my brain always finds a way to entertain itself. But this is awesome."

Arañita crawls along the same thread, not skipping to three separate thoughts or creating seven new ideas. She's focused on one thing and one thing only—the PUD.

"She . . . likes dead?" the PUD asks Benji. They rub their hands on their lap, and I watch as the skin on their palm pulls. Skin slippage usually happens two to three days after death.

Benji laughs. "Yes, she likes dead. She very much likes dead. I mean, I like dead too, but more in the form of movies and books. I may have just met her, but I'm pretty sure she likes to get all up close and personal with the dead. You're probably the best thing to ever happen to her."

A smile starts to pull at the corner of the PUD's mouth until the skin on their lip splits.

I find the chart I need in Pilar's notebook and compare it to the number of maggots in the vial. According to the chart, our PUD died eight days ago.

None of our numbers are matching up.

"We have a problem," I announce.

EIGHT

BENJI IMMEDIATELY GROANS about yet another problem on top of our growing mountain of problems while the PUD puts their head in their hands and sighs. They both probably think I'm stupid for not being able to figure all this out. Arañita is used to living human beings thinking the web in my brain is jumbled beyond repair, but an undead person is new.

Avoiding eye contact with Benji and the PUD, I collect all my data and put it together with Benji's drawing. We can't leave it lying around.

We're stuck. There's nothing else we can do until I come up with something else. But Arañita has fallen asleep, tired from focusing on one thing.

"I have an idea," Benji says, leaning in toward the PUD. "I think you came back to life because you were struck by lightning. It completely regenerated all your organs."

I raise my eyebrow and the PUD huffs. "Isn't that . . . Frankenstein?" they ask.

Benji throws his hands in the air. "It was worth a shot."

I lead the PUD to the walk-in freezer in the corner of the lab that's hardly ever used.

"You'll be safe in here," I tell them. "The temperature will help slow down your decomposition. We have to or we'll have nothing to work with."

The PUD's eyes grow wide, the red-tinged one looking like it might roll right out of their skull.

"Ouch. Harsh," Benji says.

I shake my head as I lead the PUD inside the freezer. I shiver and wrap my arms around myself. The PUD settles in the corner, pulling their knees to their chest with a grunt.

"I'm sorry," I say. Arañita messed up once again. I didn't have the answers I promised.

The PUD nods slowly.

I sit down next to them, the metal rack behind me cold against my back.

"I'm sorry this happened to you," I tell them. "I really am. Benji and I are going to figure this out."

The PUD tries to shrug their shoulders and winces. Their dark hair hangs over their forehead, and they try to flip it off their face but their neck doesn't budge.

We sit in silence and I shiver.

"Would it be okay with you if I called you a name?" I finally say. "Just so we don't keep calling you PUD?"

The PUD's lips move back and forth as if they're trying

out the word before saying it. "Name?"

I nod. "What do you think about Mateo? Or Magdalena? Or Micky? I don't know what gender we need."

The PUD looks at me, their yellow-tinged eyes searching my face. "I'm . . . a boy. And Mateo . . . good."

I hop up. "Oh, perfect. Well, it's nice to meet you, Mateo. I'm Frani, and standing outside a lot warmer is Benji. We're both twelve. I think you're just a little older than us. Like maybe high school? You don't feel like you're married with three kids and a thirty-year mortgage, do you?"

Mateo smiles and his skin stretches. "I think . . . teenage Mateo . . . is right."

I give him a thumbs-up. "We're going to help you. No matter what it takes."

Mateo shifts his weight and leans slightly against me. The feel of his bone arm and loose skin doesn't bother me. "Do you think . . . someone's looking for me?"

"Of course," I blurt out. Then I take a deep breath. "One time, Profe took me and Essie—that's my sister—to float on the Navarro River. I got distracted by some turtles that were stacked up on a log and didn't notice that Profe's and Essie's inner tubes had floated down the river away from me. Profe didn't know where I was when they got to the dock where we were supposed to be getting out of the water. I've never heard Profe shout my name so loudly."

Mateo wrings his hands in his lap but stops when his

fingers crack. "Someone is shouting . . . for me?"

"Definitely," I tell him. "We just have to figure out who they are. And who you are."

Mateo nods and slowly wraps his arms around his legs as he sits on the floor. "I'm glad . . . you found me."

I smile and exit the freezer, sealing the door behind me.

"Hiding a body in a freezer is a first for me. And while this summer is already starting to be the best I've ever had, I've gotta ask . . . now what?" Benji asks.

I sigh. "I have absolutely no idea."

NINE

I SPEND A restless night as Arañita flies all over her web. She won't calm down long enough to let me fall asleep. I think about all the data I collected from Mateo and how none of the numbers match up. I'm certain I didn't do anything wrong. But it was probably the first time the numbers were being used on a reanimated corpse.

I grumble my way through breakfast, tired and still focused on Mateo. Arañita keeps plucking that thread and won't let go. Profe told me this is called "hyperfocus," when your brain only wants to think about one thing and nothing else. I call it Arañita being annoying.

Essie sits at the kitchen table, and I bounce my leg up and down waiting for her to leave. I have to steal some of her makeup to use on Mateo. If he runs into anyone, there's no way we can hide the decomposition on his face without some assistance. Essie might straight-up murder me when she finds out I've used her foundation and powder on a corpse, but that'll make a fun epitaph for my gravestone. And she's always mad at me lately, so this won't matter much.

Profe leans over to Essie as she shows him her latest selfie with Yaikira. As she slides her finger across her phone, flipping through her photo album, Arañita plucks hard at a string.

"The cameras!" I blurt out, dropping my fork onto my plate of dry scrambled eggs.

Essie looks up and raises her eyebrow. "What are you talking about?"

I shake my head. "N-nothing. Random thought. Y-you know me," I stammer.

Essie rolls her eyes. "Yeah, I do. We're lucky you didn't blurt out 'intestines' or something."

Profe chuckles as he takes one last gulp of his coffee. "I'm off to class, niñas. Behave," Profe says with a wink, getting up from the table.

"Have fun scaring students with bloat photos," I tell him. "Oh, or maybe that one of the cadaver that was found after four days in the water. That one is awesome."

Essie sets her Pop-Tart back down on her paper towel. "Stop. I'm begging you to stop."

I wish I could tell Profe all about Mateo right there. He'd know what to do. But Essie would stop me mid-sentence and groan about how I'm always making up stories. And then we'd probably get in an argument and ruin Profe's day when he should be focusing on his classes. I'll tell Profe when I catch him alone in the lab later today. If Arañita can remember.

Once Profe and Essie leave, I race to the bathroom and grab her makeup. When I head to the lab and open the freezer, Mateo is still sitting in the same position I left him in yesterday. His skin is less yellow and has a white sheen from the cold temperature.

"Do you think you can move?" I ask him, holding out my hand as I stand above him.

Mateo slowly lifts his arm and a loud snap fills the freezer as his joints crack. "I think I'm . . . undead popcorn."

"That might be part from being frozen and part from rigor mortis."

The corner of Mateo's mouth tugs. "Both . . . not good."

I chuckle. "Yeah, you're right. But guess what? I came up with the most brilliant idea this morning. My sister was showing Profe pictures on her phone and I got to thinking about all the different ways Profe maintains security here. Did you know that one time a group of students from the university tried to steal a body as some kind of fraternity prank? I mean, how stupid. I can think of a million ways to have fun other than lugging a decomposed body around."

Mateo stares at me as he slowly stands. I can hear his muscles and joints popping. "So many . . . words," Mateo says.

I smack my forehead. "Right, sorry. One of the things

we have on the body farm for security are game cameras. You know, the ones hunters use to track deer in the forest? They're motion activated. So maybe one of the cameras caught you when you got buried in the ground. Since we already know when you popped up and grabbed me. Not gonna forget that."

"Sorry . . . about that. Undead is new . . . to me," Mateo says.

He shuffles from the freezer after I check that Dr. Tanaka and Pilar aren't anywhere.

"I've got another idea on how our PUD came back from the dead," Benji says as he comes into the lab. "It was probably an industrial accident from a pharmaceutical factory that leaked drugs into the water. Just like in my favorite movie, *Train to Busan*."

"There aren't any factories like that in San Zavala," I tell him as I head over to Profe's computer.

Benji shrugs. "Bummer."

"You . . . tried," Mateo says with a wink.

Benji holds out a gray San Zavala Zonkeys hoodie to Mateo. "I brought you some clean clothes. Dad got this for me so I'd fit in at my new school this year."

Arañita skips across a thread. Is that all it really takes? Maybe that's been my problem all these years. I just needed clothes with a zebra-donkey hybrid on them.

Mateo takes a deep breath and holds the gray hoodie up

to his ashy cheek. "At least it matches . . . me."

Benji laughs as he helps Mateo change into the hoodie. The skin on Mateo's arms sags and splits over his left elbow, exposing the bone. The freezer didn't quite work well enough.

"So is there a brilliant plan for the day?" Benji says, still staring at Mateo with wide eyes.

I click through several screens on the computer, searching for what I need. "Cameras. We can look through the cameras out in the field to see if we can spot when Mateo ended up on the rocks. Oh, he's Mateo, by the way. I figured that was better than PUD."

Benji nods as he sits next to me at the computer. "Well, Mateo's good because you aren't really a PUD anymore. More like a DUD."

"DUD?" Mateo asks.

"Definitely Undead Dude."

Mateo starts to bite his lip again but stops when I look at him.

"Found it!" I declare, clicking on the file that stores all the video from the game cameras that gets uploaded through their SIM cards. "Now we just need to find the right camera and the footage from the correct time."

We scan through the footage and watch videos of Profe, Dr. Tanaka, and Pilar checking on the cadavers in the field, taking pictures and measurements. There are a few videos of Dr. Tanaka reinforcing a cage over a cadaver that was messed up by overenthusiastic coyotes. I also spot some videos of Pilar by herself in the field, which is a little odd since she always says she doesn't like going out there alone. But Profe must've given her a task to do with her bugs.

I click on a file and spot a deer wandering through the grass just down the hill from where Winston lies.

"This is it. This is the camera we need," I say, uploading the videos from the camera that's secured to the live oak tree trunk next to Winston. "You grabbed my ankle right by the fence here. If only we could find the footage before that."

Because the camera is motion activated, there are short videos of coyotes scampering by and vultures flying down to inspect Winston. A bright red cardinal lands on the rock right in front of the camera and pecks at it.

"Where . . . am I?" Mateo asks next to me, his eyes glued to the computer.

I sigh. "I haven't seen you yet."

Benji pulls out his phone. "We should look him up on a missing persons website or something. Maybe there are people looking for you?"

Mateo opens his mouth to say something, but his body tenses and he coughs, a sharp noise shaking his spine. He covers his mouth and when he stops coughing, his eyes widen. He holds out his hand to us, revealing three teeth sitting in the middle of his palm.

Benji starts typing furiously on his phone. "Yep, we gotta do something. This whole 'body parts in my hand' show-and-tell has gotta stop."

"I . . . agree," Mateo says, sliding the teeth into the pocket of the hoodie Benji gave him. I wonder where his pinky finger ended up. "I don't like . . . being a body part puzzle."

Benji shows us his phone. "This is the website for the National Center for Missing and Exploited Children. It looks like we can search missing posters here."

Benji stands next to Mateo while I busy myself looking at more game camera videos. I find the video from when Mateo grabbed my ankle. His hand shoots up from between two rocks and Benji and I run away. But then the video ends. There should be more, assuming he kept pushing through the mesquite shrubs growing between the rocks. And there's nothing before it either. It's like it's been erased.

"This website wants to know your name and age," Benji says.

Mateo closes his eyes, searching for information in a brain that I'm afraid is starting to liquefy. "I . . . don't know. Can't remember."

Benji bites his lip and types on his phone. I pull up another camera, one farther down the hill that points along the fence line between the body farm and the agricultural center.

"I'm gonna put in the least amount of information I can

and see what comes up. I'm assuming your hair is black and your eye color is brown. That's what it looks like right now. And let's say your location is San Zavala. Hopefully you didn't travel here from anywhere else. You said your gender was male, so I'll put that in."

Mateo nods, and I watch a video of a Black Angus cow chewing a patch of grass growing along the fence line.

"Oh my god," Benji gasps.

"What?" Mateo asks. "You . . . found me?"

Benji scrolls through his phone and swallows hard. "There's just so many. So many kids."

He nudges me with his elbow, and I look away from the computer screen. "What'd you say?" I ask. Arañita was hyperfocused on the game cameras.

Benji holds out his phone and scrolls through poster after poster of missing boys with black hair and brown eyes. Most of them are Latinx, Black, and Asian. He purses his lips and his knuckles grow white as he grips his phone harder. "I said there are so many of them. Why isn't this on the news every night? Why isn't everyone out trying to find all these kids?"

Mateo raises his finger to Benji's phone, his nail jagged and the skin tightly stretched across his knuckle.

"Maybe . . . we don't . . . matter," he says, his hand dropping to his lap as he sighs.

Arañita plucks at a string and I blurt out, "I read that the news covers missing white kids more than Brown and Black kids, even though we're more likely to go missing."

Benji slams his phone down on the desk and I jump. "That's a load of rotten hamburger."

"Can we post about Mateo on that website?" I ask.

Benji clicks through and shakes his head. "It seems like only law enforcement can add new posts. Besides, they want us to upload a current picture, but I don't think we should do that."

Mateo reaches a four-fingered hand up to his face—the skin around his eyes red and sagging, his teeth missing, and a lone maggot crawling out of his ear. "Not . . . my best look," he says.

I shake my head. "Nope. Definitely not."

Drumming my fingers on the desk, I think as Arañita bounces across one thread and over to another.

"I could just show him pictures, I guess," I mumble.

Benji looks at me. "What was the first part of that sentence?"

I shake my head. "Oh, um, I have an idea about where we could post Mateo's information. But we need to know more about him."

I type in a new website and the Story Stack logo fills the screen. I click the "start a new story" button.

As Benji scans his drawing, I turn to Mateo. "We need to figure out what you like and don't like. Since you can't really remember anything, I thought maybe I'd show you pictures. Just tell me if they seem like something you were into when you were alive."

Mateo's lip twitches slightly when I say *alive*, but he nods slowly. "I'll try. It's still . . . a black hole . . . in my head."

Opening a new tab on the computer, I show him a picture of a large, gooey cheese pizza.

"Yes," he says, smiling slightly.

Benji clears his throat. "Everyone likes pizza, Frani. That's not going to narrow it down at all."

I shrug. "Fine."

I pull up a picture of a pizza with pineapple and black olives on it.

"No . . . definitely no." Mateo says quickly.

Chuckling, Benji says, "Again, everybody has that opinion. Neither of these things make him unique or stand out."

"Fine," I groan. "What about this?"

A YouTube video of a skateboarder riding a rail in front of a building plays on the computer screen. Mateo's eyes grow wide, the yellow parts filling with twisty red blood vessels.

"I think . . . I really liked that," he says. His index and ring finger tap on his leg again.

I smile. "Thought so. That move you keep doing with your fingers on your leg is exactly what kids at school do when they're playing with those mini skateboards on their desks. Right before the teachers take them away."

We spend the next several minutes clicking through pictures on the computer. Mateo smiles and nods when I show him pictures of pan dulce, a corgi, and a picture of CTU students swimming in the river that flows through campus. He grimaces and shakes his head when he sees a jar full of fiery salsa, a black cat riding on top of a robot vacuum, and a stack of old books.

I try to figure out the family that might be missing him, so I show him pictures of a kid with two sisters and a mom and dad, a kid with no siblings and two moms, and twin boys with a sister and two dads. Mateo's lips press together and he looks down, scratching his jagged nails along his dusty jeans. He doesn't seem to have an opinion about any of them.

Taking a deep breath, I begin writing on Story Stack. Arañita crawls to a stop, no longer distracted by the threads she was following with each picture that popped up on the computer.

This may be a different story than what's usually posted on this site, but I need everyone's help. The other day, I met a new friend named Mateo. He doesn't remember who he is or where he came from. His name isn't even Mateo. I made that up for him.

But I do know some things about him. He likes

skateboarding. Who knows? He might even be pretty good at it. He thinks that yellow conchas are better than mantecadas, and I agree. I'm pretty sure he likes swimming and is maybe not that excited about reading old books in school. He likes dogs better than cats and sweet foods better than spicy ones.

He was found sitting in front of the math department building at Central Texas University on July 24 wearing a red hoodie and jeans. He has a dry sense of humor and his left eye closes more than his right when he smiles. He likes to bite his lip a lot. We want to get him back to the people who love him.

After I scan and upload Benji's drawing, I hit "submit" and give Mateo a thumbs-up.

"This is just a storytelling website my English teacher showed us. A lot of other schools in the district use it too. I don't have many followers but maybe someone will recognize you and have information about who you are," I tell him.

He takes a deep breath and nods. "Thank . . . you."

I turn back to the computer and click on another video saved in the lab's archive. In between a row of pecan trees, three stakes stick up from the ground, marking the three cadavers buried there. One is set on the ground, a cage over its body so animals don't disturb it. The second is completely buried, a soft mound of earth rising next to the stake. And the third is partially buried, the top half of its body lying on the sandy dirt. I squint, wondering what movement made the camera turn on and start recording.

And then I see it.

The fingers on the third cadaver wiggle slightly, stretching and reaching. At first, I think it's just a trick of the light or the bugs under the dirt causing the movement. But the cadaver's mouth opens, revealing missing teeth that probably fell to the back of their throat five days after they were placed in the field.

Suddenly, they sit up.

I gasp.

Benji's mouth drops open. "Frani, what's the time stamp on that? When did it happen?"

I look in the corner of the screen and my heart jumps into my throat.

With a shaking finger, I point to the time.

"Only thirty minutes ago. This just happened."

TEN

MY PHONE RINGS and I pull it from my back pocket.

It's Profe, so I answer and put it on speaker.

"Oye, Frani. All hands on deck. Dr. Tanaka just reported a cadaver missing. Are you in the lab?" Profe says. He sounds out of breath.

"Yep. We're here and doing totally normal stuff. Promise," I say, trying to make my voice sound as calm as possible, but it comes out in a high-pitched squeak.

"I need you to bring the drone to Cadaver 072201's location. I'll meet you there," Profe says, and hangs up before I can agree.

Benji hops up from his stool. "Is that the same body we saw on the computer?"

I nod. "Profe will want to track it. We can all go out there and help, but we'll need to help cover up Mateo a little bit. You're looking too . . . ripe. And Profe seems like he's dealing with a lot of stress right now. He's probably surrounded by all his assistants. Plus, campus police might already be involved. I won't have a chance to get him alone and make him understand what's going on."

Standing over Mateo, I pull out Essie's foundation, dumping a little of the liquid on my hand. I take my fingers and brush them over Mateo's cheek. His skin pulls underneath my hand and tears, a long rip from under his right eye to the corner of his mouth. Bright red muscle peeks out from the gap like a bundle of string.

"Oh . . . oops," I blurt out.

"Oops? I'm not . . . pretty anymore?" Mateo asks, and then winks at me, his eyelids sticking together.

Holding out a mask from the box on the table to Mateo, Benji says, "This will work better than Frani's makeup nightmare. Just keep it on and your hoodie up. Hands in your pockets. I think that covers all our bases."

"Don't drop any body parts either," I blurt. *Shut up, Arañita.*

Mateo smiles slightly before he covers his mouth with the face mask. "I'll . . . try my best . . . to not leave . . . a trail of fingers and toes."

I grab the case that has the drone Profe needs and we head out into the field. The sun is strong, and Benji and I immediately start sweating.

I look at Mateo as he shuffles along with us. Not one bead of sweat drips down his skin as he's bundled under his thick hoodie and long pants. That's going to be hard to explain, but Profe will be more preoccupied with the missing cadaver.

Oh, maggot nostrils. The missing cadaver.

The cadaver that's not exactly missing because we saw it wake up and pop out of the ground. How do I even begin to tell Profe that?

Scurrying down the hill as quickly as we can while still letting Mateo keep up with us, we finally arrive at Cadaver 072201's spot, next to the two other cadavers between the row of pecan trees. Except Cadaver 072201 isn't there. The dirt is loose around the shallow hole where they should be and Pilar crouches over it, picking at the ground with tweezers. Beads of sweat drip down her arm, making it look like the tattoo on her bicep is crying.

"I've got the drone," I say, holding the case out to Profe. His eyes immediately fall on Mateo and my stomach flip-flops. Arañita races across her thread, trying to come up with an explanation for the slightly decomposed person next to us.

"This is Mateo. He's a friend from school. I wanted Benji to meet him so he'd know more kids when school starts."

Profe nods and wipes sweat off his forehead with the back of his hand. I doubt he believes me. I never have friends over. I don't even have friends. "Thanks, Frani."

Benji steps up to Profe. "Can I help, sir?"

Profe smiles and nods. "Of course. Your dad tells me you're the champion of *Brain Bashers 3*. I need an expert at my controls."

Benji laughs, and he and Profe start setting up the drone. I head over to Pilar, and Mateo follows me.

"Tracking the bugs?" I ask, walking up behind her.

Pilar jumps and quickly shoves a vial into her pocket. She stands up and faces us, blowing sweaty bangs off her forehead.

"You know it, Frani Fran!" she says, a little too enthusiastically. "I couldn't pass up the chance to document what kind of bugs were present and in what numbers. That's just the sort of thing we love at the Dirt Nap Motel, right?"

Pilar looks Mateo up and down and cocks her head to the side, an eyebrow raised. Mateo shuffles his feet in the dirt, his gaze on the ground.

"Did you ever find that bug you were missing?" I ask, hoping to distract her from Mateo.

Pilar groans and runs her fingers through her hair. "No, it's still running around here somewhere. You let me know if you spot it. And don't smush it."

A whirring sound fills the air, and we all look up. The drone flies overhead, searching for the missing cadaver.

"No luck, Profe," a voice calls. Dr. Tanaka comes trudging up the hill from the tree line. "No sign of the body, at least not close by."

When he reaches us, he shakes his head. "I can't believe an animal would've dragged it so far. They're usually only a few feet away when that happens."

"Nothing's showing up on the drone either," Profe says, his hands on his hips as he leans over Benji's shoulder and watches the screen on the drone controller.

Luckily everyone is so preoccupied with the missing cadaver that none of them pays much attention to Mateo standing next to me. He scuffs his feet in the dirt and nudges me with his elbow, as his hands are shoved in his pockets.

"Frani?" he whispers.

I pull him away from the others as Pilar and Dr. Tanaka walk over to Profe. "What?"

"That . . . will happen . . . to me?"

I follow Mateo's gaze to the cadaver lying under the metal cage. They've been out in the elements long enough that their hair mat has slid into the dirt. Their skin has slipped from their thighs, exposing the muscle underneath. Their teeth and eyes have disappeared. Anyone else would think this is a disgusting horror story or a terrible Halloween costume.

But it's just scientific fact.

I shrug. "Yes. That's what happens to all dead bodies as they decompose. It's normal."

Mateo's breathing speeds up and his eyes dart up and

down the hill. His mask has fallen under his chin, and he bites his lip. Before I can stop him, he pushes his teeth clear through the skin.

"No . . . no," he mumbles as his hands shake at his sides. His missing pinky finger is clearly visible, and I stand between him and the adults, blocking their view.

I clench my fists. I shouldn't have blurted out what I did. I should've found a nicer way to break the news to Mateo. But Arañita pushes the first thing that pops into my head out of my mouth without waiting for me to consider whether it's actually the right thing to say.

"I'm sorry," I tell Mateo. I reach to put my hand on his shoulder, but he shuffles backward.

He hunches over and before I can try to come up with something better to say to him, I hear Profe on his phone.

"Captain Reynolds?" Profe says, his voice the most serious I've ever heard it. "We've got a problem over here at the facility. A cadaver's missing. I'm not sure if it's a student prank, but we can't find the body anywhere in the vicinity."

Profe watches Benji pack up the drone as he listens to whatever Captain Reynolds is telling him.

"Okay, well, we'll need your resources on it as soon as you can spare them," he finally responds. He thanks Captain Reynolds and hangs up.

“What’s the problem?” Dr. Tanaka asks as he scrolls through the iPad in his hands.

Profe slides his phone into his back pocket. “I think CTU has reached an all-time high for pranks. Captain Reynolds said a woman just wandered onto the football practice field and tried to attack the players.”

Pilar’s eyes grow wide as she shoves her hands into her pockets. “Did he say what she looked like?”

Profe shrugs. “Other than her wearing some kind of strange costume, no, he didn’t. It looks like we’re on our own trying to find the body until the university police department is finished dealing with that mess.”

Mateo’s breathing is still increasing. I watch him shake his head. “No . . . no,” he keeps muttering under his breath.

“Lower your voice,” I whisper. I don’t want him drawing attention to himself.

Luckily, Profe, Dr. Tanaka, and Pilar head back to the lab, discussing methods to find the body.

“What’s wrong?” Benji asks, walking over to us and pointing to Mateo.

Mateo stumbles back, his eyes still fixed on the cadaver lying under the cage. “I can’t . . . be that,” he says. “I can’t.”

Benji approaches him, but Mateo holds his hand up. “No . . . stay away.”

“Why? We’re your friends,” Benji says.

Mateo shuffles away from us farther. "Don't get . . . near me."

I put my hands on my hips. "Why don't you want us to figure things out? We can help you."

Mateo's eyes snap to me. His upper lip curls, revealing jagged teeth, and he takes a deep, shuddering breath.

"Because . . . I'm hungry."

ELEVEN

BENJI TAKES A step back. "What does that mean?"

Mateo doubles over and puts his hands on his knees. "I can hear . . . your heartbeat."

I put my hand on Mateo's shoulder, but he bolts upright, the quickest I've ever seen him move. His eyes flash red, the blood vessels bursting. "No . . . stay away."

His gaze snaps to us and a growl grows from his throat. His eyes widen in horror, and he stumbles down the hill, into the tree line. I start to follow him, but Benji grabs my arm.

"No, Frani. I don't think we should go after him," he says. "It's not safe."

I wrench my arm from Benji's grip. "But we have to help him."

Running to the trees, I trip over rocks and dodge cacti sprouting from the ground. Quickly out of breath, I scan the woods and spot Mateo shuffling between two mesquite bushes. His feet catch on a rock, and he stumbles to the ground.

I run over to him and crouch at his side.

"Are you okay?" I ask, placing my hand on his arm. I can feel the bone beneath the sleeve of his hoodie.

"Get away . . . from me. I don't want . . . to hurt you," Mateo mumbles, trying to free his arm from my grip but too weak to do so.

I take a deep breath and help Mateo to his feet. "I don't think you're going to hurt me. You wouldn't do that."

Mateo examines my face. His eyes are red and dark bruises sit under his eye sockets. "I feel . . . weird. Different."

I chuckle. "Well, I feel like that every day, and it doesn't make me want to eat anyone."

Benji runs up to us, his breath catching in his throat. His shoulders heave and he puts his hands on his hips. "It's too hot to run. I mean, I don't like to run in any kind of weather, but it's not smart to do it when it's a gajillion degrees outside."

He looks from Mateo to me and bites his lip. "So, everybody okay here? No strange food cravings?"

Mateo takes a deep breath and slowly puts his hands in his pockets. "I think . . . I'm okay now."

"Maggot nostrils," I say.

Benji raises an eyebrow. "What? You don't believe him?"

I shake my head. "No. That's not it. Look at what Mateo tripped over."

I point at a shallow hole in the ground in front of us, the dirt and rocks loose around it. The wooden stake at the edge with a metal tag stuck to it, reading Cadaver 122305.

"Does that mean what I think it means?" Benji asks.

I nod slowly and sigh. "Yep. Another cadaver is missing."

Benji groans. "So three cadavers have decided to go topside and join the living. Why is this happening?"

Mateo reaches out a shaky finger and pokes me in the arm to get my attention. "What if . . . they're hungry too?"

I purse my lips as I think. Sweat drips down my forehead and pools on my upper lip. Arañita takes off bouncing across her web.

"Butterscotch candies really are the worst, aren't they?" I blurt out.

Benji looks at me and a smile breaks out on his face. "Keep going."

I chuckle. Benji isn't like the kids at school. He doesn't seem to be bothered by Arañita. She flew over fifteen threads before landing on the butterscotch string. But explaining the whole journey is too frustrating. Arañita doesn't want to retrace her steps. She's already jumped three threads ahead. "We should go see Captain Reynolds."

"Isn't that the guy who's a little busy with the whole costumed lady versus the football team thing?" Benji starts following me down the hill to the agriculture center gate that leads to campus. "Don't you think we should do the opposite of introducing our DUD friend to the local law enforcement?"

"Maybe," I say. "But he'll have access to databases about missing people that we don't. We might not know why all these DUDs are strolling around, but we can still figure out who Mateo really is."

Mateo looks at me with a smile that stretches and cracks his lips. "Good . . . plan."

We walk as quickly as Mateo can through the agricultural center and onto campus. Several students are putting up welcome banners. We've got to figure out this whole DUD situation before the university is flooded with new students. I sneak glances at Mateo as he keeps his head down, covered by his hoodie, and his hands in his pockets.

"I think I know why you and all these DUDs are popping up," Benji says as we pass two girls taping Student Pescatarian Association flyers to light poles.

"What is it . . . now?" Mateo chuckles.

Benji claps. "I got it. So the body farm actually sits on top of a cursed cemetery and the ghosts of the bodies there are infesting all the cadavers and bringing them back to life."

"I'm . . . possessed?" Mateo tries to raise his eyebrow but his skin starts to pull and tear. "Awesome."

I shake my head. "I'm pretty sure none of that is true.

Something is definitely happening on the body farm. I don't know what it is, but Profe always tells me I should focus on what I can control. It keeps me from getting overwhelmed. And we should focus on Mateo."

Mateo smiles. "I'm okay . . . with that plan. I'm good . . . being focused on."

When we get to the CTU police department, I grab Mateo's arm to stop him. I hear a pop as his forearm dislocates from his elbow.

"Sorry," I say. "But I think it's probably best if you wait out here. I'm not sure how we'd explain you to Captain Reynolds."

Mateo nods. He glances over to a group of students setting up a table with a sign that reads *CTU Naked Paintball Club*. "Safe . . . out here?"

Chuckling, Benji winks. "Just don't talk to anyone. Or look at anyone. Or breathe in anyone's general direction."

He sounds like Arañita preparing me for the first day of school.

Mateo sits on a bench outside the building as Benji and I go through the main doors. The desk sergeant looks confused as she hangs up the phone at the desk with a "No, I don't have any more information about a woman challenging the whole football team to a fight."

I recognize her from the last time we needed help locating a body that had gone missing. She threw up three times as we searched through the body farm because coyotes dragged away a cadaver.

"Hi, Sergeant Cho. We're here to see Captain Reynolds," I tell her.

Sergeant Cho chuckles. "He'll probably welcome a distraction, Frani. It's been quite the afternoon."

She buzzes us through the door, and we head down to Captain Reynolds's office. When I knock, a voice calls back, "As long as you're not here to tell me another fool is running around campus tackling people, come on in."

Benji and I laugh as we enter.

"Frani!" Captain Reynolds says as he turns his chair away from his computer. The dark brown skin of his left arm is entirely covered with a tattoo of a longhorn cow. When he transferred from the San Zavala Police Department to the university, Profe said he made a lot of good changes—he worked with the university to have more mental health resources for students and support for underprivileged students. The department's officers don't even carry guns.

I always feel comfortable around him. Even though he has bad taste in candy, at least the shelves in his office are lined with Funko Pops! of comic book characters.

"Hey, Captain," I say, sitting down in one of the two chairs across from his desk.

"Tell your dad I'm rounding up some officers to help with his missing cadaver as soon as they're done with this whole football player debacle. I've been on the phone all day with the dean of every department telling me student orientation is in two weeks and we can't have people running around attacking kids. Like I didn't already know that."

He slides a glass dish filled with butterscotch candies across his desk to me and Benji.

Benji sits in the chair next to me and winks, realizing the connection I made in our conversation earlier.

"We actually came to ask you for help with something else," I tell Captain Reynolds.

"Not a lady in an adult-sized Pikachu onesie?"

I clench my fists. "What? Is that what the woman was wearing?"

Captain Reynolds nods. "Yep. Do you know her?"

I shake my head and look at Benji. He's only known me a couple of days, but he can already tell when Arañita is lying. I'd focus on how good it feels for someone to finally understand me if I wasn't preoccupied with recognizing the woman in the Pokémon pajamas—she's one of the cadavers in Dr. Tanaka's study.

Captain Reynolds unwraps a butterscotch candy and pops it in his mouth, crunching down on it immediately. "So what do you kids need?"

I wipe my sweaty palms on the legs of my shorts. "Benji and I were doing research about how minority kids are less likely to get media coverage when they go missing in comparison to white kids."

Captain Reynolds's eyebrows knit together, and he purses his lips. Taking a deep breath, he says, "That's unfortunately true. I was on several cases when I worked for the city. They didn't have resources to communicate with families that didn't speak English. The files got shuffled from desk to desk. Meanwhile, whole candlelight vigils and search parties were organized for other children."

Benji grips the arms of his chair. "That's not fair."

Captain Reynolds nods. "You're right. It's not."

"Do you have a database that keeps information about missing kids?" I ask.

Captain Reynolds turns to his computer and clicks on the screen. "Well, there's the National Center for Missing and Exploited Children—"

"We've looked at that," I interrupt. *Rude, Arañita.* "Sorry."

Captain Reynolds nods again. "I also have access to more local databases. Are you looking for anything specific or do you just want general information?"

I look at Benji, unsure how to get what we want without telling Captain Reynolds that our missing person is a reanimated corpse who's sitting right outside the building.

Benji squares his shoulders. "Um, let's say that you only had a little bit of information about someone, like you didn't even know their name, and you were trying to figure out who they were. Would those local registries be able to give you results if you only knew bits and pieces?"

Captain Reynolds raises his eyebrow. "Like you've got someone who doesn't remember who they are?"

I shrug casually, trying to look nonchalant. "Sure. Could we see how that would work?"

Captain Reynolds pulls up a website on his computer with Cerro County at the top. "I think it's possible. So, what could we say we know about this person?"

Benji winks at me. "Well, they're a boy. He has black hair and brown eyes. He's five feet eleven inches tall. And he's probably between twelve and eighteen years old."

Captain Reynolds types the information into the fields on the website. After a few moments, we get some results.

"How many?" I ask, glancing over Captain Reynolds's shoulder.

"Seems like with just those bits, we've got ten results."

I look at Benji with wide eyes and he gives me a thumbs-up.

"Do you mind if we look through them?" I ask. "I was wondering what that kind of database looked like."

Captain Reynolds stands. "I gotta get up. Been on the phone all morning dealing with an angry football coach and pesky news reporters, so I need to stretch my legs."

He motions me to his chair and I sit down, clicking through the results. Three of them are Black boys. Even with the amount of decomposition that's happened on Mateo's skin, it's obvious he's not Black. Another kid is white but he has a scar on his chin that Mateo doesn't have. The other six results are Latino boys. Benji stands behind me as I click through the pictures.

Two of the boys have short curly hair that doesn't look anything like Mateo's. Another has braces on his teeth. And a fourth looks like he weighs forty pounds more than Mateo. But then I click on the next result.

A boy stares back at me, his brow furrowed as his black hair falls across his forehead. His lips are in a tight line. He doesn't look happy to have his picture taken.

But he looks exactly like Mateo. He's even wearing a red hoodie.

Benji nudges my shoulder. "It's him!" he whispers too loudly.

"You know one of these kids?" Captain Reynolds asks.

"Um . . . I think maybe this one," I say, pointing to the screen. Arañita doesn't know what else to say.

I read the information on the screen. My heartbeat pounds in my ears and my leg bounces up and down uncontrollably under Captain Reynolds's desk.

Santiago Aguilar, age 16. Reported missing on July 25.

We found him.

TWELVE

I LEAN CLOSER to the computer, not hearing Benji and Captain Reynolds talk behind me. Their voices are muffled out by Arañita's focus on the screen. I take in all the information in the file about Santiago Aguilar.

He was reported missing by a teacher, Reina Salgado, at San Zavala High School on July 25. There's nothing about family. The teacher made a statement to the San Zavala police and I click on the file. It's a scanned page of the teacher's loopy, careful handwriting.

Santiago hasn't been in my summer school math class for an entire week, since July 20. My colleagues at the high school aren't worried because he usually doesn't have the best attendance. I went to visit his foster family and they told me they hadn't seen him in four days. They said not to worry because, according to them, he runs off a lot. None of the kids I've seen him hang around with at school have heard from him. They say he doesn't have a cell phone. I think he's missing.

I pick at the cuticle on my left thumb as I read the statement over and over. I picture Mateo—I mean, Santiago—slumped in his seat in Reina Salgado's class, his red hoodie pulled over his head. He's bored because he already knows all the answers. The only reason he's in summer school is because he never went to class during the regular school year and missed all the tests. And he's not happy about this fact.

"Right, Frani?" I hear Captain Reynolds's voice behind me.

I shake my head, settling Arañita into place so I can focus on what he's saying.

"Could you repeat that, sir?" I say.

"I was just telling your friend Benji here that if y'all know anything about this kid, let me know so we can find him. Nobody should be lost," Captain Reynolds says.

I nod. "Yes, sir. But could you tell me if the police did anything with this report?"

Captain Reynolds leans over my shoulder and takes the computer mouse, scrolling through the information about Santiago.

He sighs. "It doesn't look like it."

“What would you have done?” Benji asks.

Captain Reynolds stands back up and crosses his arms. The longhorn tattoo on his bicep flexes. “There’s a lot they could’ve done. Interviewed the foster family more. Talked to his classmates to find out where he usually hangs out. Interviewed the child services caseworker about him. Anything’s better than just letting a file sit on a desk.”

Benji nods as I get up from the computer. “Anything is always better than nothing.”

“Thanks for letting us use your computer,” I tell Captain Reynolds. “Sorry about your busy morning.”

I think about the two empty graves at the body farm, their former occupants possibly roaming around the university.

“Um,” I say, clearing my throat. “Be careful out there today, sir. Seems like there’s some strange stuff going on.”

Captain Reynolds smiles and takes a card from his desk, writing on the back of it. “Look, I’m gonna be honest with you kids,” he says. “I feel like you’re not telling me everything about what’s happening. And that’s fine. I get it. But if you decide to let me know anything about this kid at all that would help us find him, call me on this number here. He deserves to be found.”

Benji takes the card from Captain Reynolds. “Thank you, sir.”

“Hope the rest of your day is free of Pikachus roaming

around," I tell him as we leave his office. Captain Reynolds's laughter bounces down the hallway as we push through the doors of the police department.

The sun is much lower in the sky than when we first left the body farm, casting long shadows over the brick walkways on campus.

"Wow, we were in there a lot longer than I thought," I say. Arañita is an expert at losing track of time.

Mateo stands up when he sees us. "Any . . . luck?"

"All the luck!" I blurt out. "We know who you are!"

Mateo stands up straighter and his ragged breath catches in his throat. "Really? Am I . . . famous? Oh no . . . am I . . . a theater kid?"

Benji laughs. "Your name is Santiago Aguilar. You're sixteen years old and you went to San Zavala High School."

Mateo's, or I guess Santiago's, hands shake at his sides as he takes in what Benji is telling him. He looks at me as his lips quiver. "But . . . what happened . . . to me?"

I sit down on the bench in front of the police department, and Benji and Santiago settle on either side.

"Your math teacher, Reina Salgado, reported you missing on July twenty-fifth," I say.

Santiago closes his eyes as if he's trying to remember someone who's hiding in the most remote part of his brain.

"So no . . . factory accident? No . . . mutating virus?" he asks, his fingers gripping the worn fabric of his pants.

Benji is quiet next to me. He sighs as he picks at a loose thread on his shorts. "I wish. Those might be better than the actual truth."

I examine Benji's face and see tears pooling in the corners of his eyes. A warm breeze picks up and blows my hair into my face. I shake my head, not wanting Arañita to make up any stories about all the kids we saw in Captain Reynolds's database or Santiago's foster family. I don't want to imagine what could have brought him to the fence line between the agricultural center and the body farm. But it's no use and she spirals, weaving images that I have to close my eyes and shake my head to keep from seeing.

"I don't . . . remember," Santiago says. "I wish . . . I could remember."

Benji puts his hand gently on Santiago's back. "At least you have us now," he says.

I take a deep breath, my mind clearing at the sound of Benji's voice.

"So now that we know who you are, what do we do next?" I ask, drumming my fingers on my leg.

Benji shrugs. "Well, I guess a big problem with figuring out what to do is that we have no idea how you became a DUD."

Santiago nods. "Or what to do . . . now that I am . . . a DUD."

We sit in silence as a breeze blows through the trees.

Suddenly, Benji hops up from the bench and runs over to a live oak tree near the chemistry building. At the base of the trunk are a bunch of discarded Frisbees and soccer balls. He reaches down and grabs something, running back to us.

"You know what I like to do when my brain is stuck? Skateboard," he says, holding out a beat-up skateboard to us.

Santiago stares at the skateboard, the corners of his mouth lifting as the cut on his cheek stretches.

"Do you think . . . I could try?" he asks softly.

Benji smiles. "Of course! I'm pretty sure you knew how to do this when you were alive."

"We'll make sure you don't get hurt," I tell him as Benji and I stand on either side of Santiago, the skateboard at his feet.

"I'm already . . . dead. I don't think . . . I can get hurt more," he says.

Benji and I lightly hold Santiago's arms as he steps onto the skateboard. "Either way," Benji says, "we'll make sure you don't drop body parts across campus like the world's worst bread-crumb trail."

Santiago takes a deep breath as we guide him forward. The skateboard wheels clack on the pavement as we wind through campus. I grip the fabric of Santiago's sleeve instead of his arm because I'm afraid my fingers might go through his skin.

A chuckle rises from Santiago's throat as his smile grows wider and the skateboard speeds up. Benji and I jog to keep up.

"Did we ever decide how we're going to stop?" I ask, getting out of breath.

"Doesn't matter . . . this is the best," Santiago says as he lifts his head, the breeze blowing the top of his hoodie off his hair.

I watch his face. For a moment, he's not a DUD. He's not someone who got lost and didn't have anyone looking for him. Instead, he's Santiago, a kid who likes skateboarding, is pretty good at math, and has a great sense of humor.

Santiago's laughter still echoes off the sidewalk as we slowly bring the skateboard to a stop in front of the library. Benji and I help him off and his smile is still plastered to his face.

"Thanks," he says. "That's the best thing . . . that's happened in a while."

I open my mouth to respond but a soft growl fills the air. At first, I think it's a coyote brave enough to wander into the middle of campus. But the noise gets louder and we look around for the source.

The growl is soon followed by a shuffling sound, and the skin on the back of my neck tingles.

I squint and look down a walkway that leads into the

library. There's a figure standing at the bottom of a set of stairs. They shuffle toward us, their steps jerky and uneven.

"What is that?" Benji asks.

The figure moves closer, and we can see them more clearly.

It's a man in a light blue tuxedo and white frilly shirt.

His stringy blond hair has fallen off in patches on his scalp, leaving red marks. Skin is gone from his hands and left cheek. He's barefoot and missing three toes.

He's from the body farm. There's no doubt.

THIRTEEN

"OH NO. NOT another one," Benji says, stepping backward.

The DUD snarls but his teeth are completely gone. He stumbles toward us, and I fall into Benji as I retreat. We crash to the ground in a tangle of limbs. Santiago stands frozen, staring at the DUD with wide eyes and taking in his decomposed form.

The DUD keeps coming forward, his eyes filled with red from burst blood vessels.

"What do we do?" Benji asks, pulling me up from the ground. "Run?"

"Fire extinguisher," I say, breathless, knowing Arañita isn't making any sense to anyone else.

The DUD lifts his arms, and two fingers are missing from his right hand. He reaches out, his face straining in a grimace as he stumbles, almost losing his balance.

Santiago steps between me and the DUD, the bones in his hand cracking as he makes a fist. "Stay . . . away," he growls.

Benji takes me by the arm and leads me away from the approaching man, but I wrench myself free from his grip.

"No. We can't leave him here. He might hurt students. We've got to figure out how to stop him," I say, grabbing Santiago's arm. My fingers sink into his skin.

We scramble up the library steps, away from the DUD. I help Santiago maneuver the stairs as his muscles tighten and he loses his balance. The DUD lets out a pained howl as his feet smack into the steps. Running to the main doors of the library, we throw ourselves against the glass, causing the sensor for the automatic doors to click. The doors slide open, and we fall inside before they close behind us. Through the glass, we can still hear the DUD grunt at the bottom of the steps.

"Now . . . what?" Santiago asks, and then a smirk creeps across his cracked lips. "Do we feed him . . . a squirrel? Or the librarian?"

"Does that sound good to you?" Benji snaps his gaze to Santiago.

I search around the library. It's practically empty. If there are any students here, they're probably asleep in a study cubicle somewhere. "We need something to bop the DUD on the head with, I guess."

Benji chuckles. "A fire extinguisher? That's what you meant before, right? I'm starting to figure out your secret code."

A muffled growl fills the air, and my eyes widen as I watch the DUD push himself to the top of the stairs and stand. A tear in his pants reveals that the skin on his knee is completely gone, his white kneecap sticking through the fabric. He shuffles forward, his eyes still fixed on us.

"The doors are shut. We're okay," Benji says. He races over to a bookshelf and pulls down a thick encyclopedia.

The DUD shuffles to the library entrance and his body smacks against the doors.

"We're . . . fine," Santiago says.

The automatic sensor clicks, and the doors slide open.

"Oh, maggot nostrils," I groan.

The DUD shuffles inside the library, his feet sliding on the slick tile floor. He reaches his arms out again, the skin hanging from his hands. I look at Benji as all color drains from his face and he swallows hard.

"Book!" I shout.

Benji tosses me a heavy encyclopedia with a grunt, and it smacks against my chest. I grip it in my hands and raise my arms above my head. The DUD snaps his gaze to me and snarls, spit dripping from his gummy mouth.

I launch the book as hard as I can at the DUD's head. It slams into his forehead, splitting the skin across his skull. His neck snaps backward and for a moment I'm afraid his head is going to fall clean off his body. Instead, the DUD takes three stumbling steps away from us and falls. The back of his head smacks into the library tile with a sharp crack that makes my stomach roll.

The grunting stops. The DUD lies still on the floor.

Benji and I warily approach him. Santiago stays back, staring at the thick black substance pooling on the floor behind the DUD's head. My eyes grow wide as a single shiny beetle skitters from the crack in the DUD's skull and across the floor, leaving tiny footprints.

Without thinking, I grab a trifold brochure from the library's circulation desk and slide the beetle into it, trapping it between the folds.

Benji pulls a card from his back pocket and holds it out to me with a shaking hand.

I sigh and take out my phone, dialing the number on the card.

When the call finally connects, I say, "Hi, Captain Reynolds. Remember when I said I hoped the rest of your day was free of strangely dressed people roaming around? Well, I've got bad news for you."

FOURTEEN

CAPTAIN REYNOLDS AND Profe stand over the body lying on the floor of the library, their hands on their hips.

"Huh," Captain Reynolds says, rubbing his chin. "This is a new one for me."

Profe sighs and runs his fingers through his hair. "Me too. They don't usually wander off."

I may have temporarily stunned Profe when I finally was able to explain DUDs, and now I'm a little nervous that introducing him to Santiago will be his breaking point.

When Profe, Pilar, and Captain Reynolds got to the library, I told Santiago to hide between two bookshelves until I could figure out how to introduce him. He's been waiting awhile.

Captain Reynolds and Profe have stared at the DUD without saying anything for the past fifteen minutes.

The librarian who came up to the circulation desk right after I smacked the DUD in the forehead with an encyclopedia has finally stopped screaming. She's sitting at her desk with her head in her hands, mumbling something about being ten years past ready to retire.

Arañita speeds along her web, bouncing from thread to thread, as I watch Pilar take a thick black body bag and lay it next to the DUD. She crouches down and examines its cracked skull. I've never seen her willingly get this close to a cadaver before.

Captain Reynolds puts his hands on his hips and looks at Benji and me. "Okay, Frani. Explain to me again exactly what happened."

I take a deep breath and try to put the events in order of me and Benji fighting the DUD. But Arañita won't walk in a straight line and keeps bouncing all over the place. I clench my fists at my sides and shake my head. My breath quickens as I get more and more frustrated.

Benji clears his throat. "I can tell you, sir. If it's okay with Frani."

Starting with us leaving the campus police station, Benji explains about the DUD appearing near the library and following us inside. When he tells them about the DUD cracking his head open on the tile floor and a beetle crawling out, I hand Profe the brochure with the bug tucked inside. He unfolds the brochure and looks at the bug with a raised eyebrow. Turning to his equipment pack, he slides the beetle into a vial and seals the lid, handing it to Pilar.

She examines the bug quietly, slipping it into her pocket.

"Do you know what kind of bug that is?" I ask her.

She shrugs and looks up at the ceiling. "Have you ever been on the third floor of this library? They say it's haunted."

Immediately, Arañita races over threads, imagining books flying off shelves and bony hands tickling sleeping students.

Captain Reynolds looks from Benji to me and then quickly to the DUD before shaking his head. "Okay, forgive me for assuming anything, but y'all don't seem that shocked that this . . . person was wandering around campus looking like the zombie movies I refuse to watch."

"Oh, you really should watch them, sir. My favorite is *Valley of the Dead*," I blurt out, snapping out of my haunted library trance.

Benji nudges me with his elbow. "Not the time," he whispers.

I scuff my feet on the floor. Profe looks at me and coughs.

"Frani, is there something you're not telling us?" he asks. He knows me better than anyone. Arañita can't hide anything from him.

I take a deep breath and square my shoulders. "There's someone I need to introduce you to."

Turning and facing Santiago's hiding spot between the bookshelves, I call out, "Santiago? It's okay. You can come out now."

A gray-hooded head peeks out from between the shelves.

Santiago shuffles over to us with his usual habit of keeping his head down and his hands in his pockets. But he's not wearing a face mask like he was when he was out in the field with everyone. The large gash that runs across his cheek is clearly visible.

A small yelp erupts from Captain Reynolds's throat. Pilar's eyes grow wide and she shoves her hands into her pockets. Profe's voice fills the empty library. "Qué tontería es eso?"

"I can explain," I say, tugging on the sleeve of Santiago's hoodie and pulling him next to me. He looks at me with nervous eyes.

"I sure hope so," Captain Reynolds says, staring at Santiago and swallowing hard.

I try my best, but Arañita blurts out a word flood all about Santiago grabbing my leg, and Benji and me trying to help him figure out who he is. She tops it off with confessing that we hid Santiago in the laboratory freezer and that we found out who he really is in Captain Reynolds's database. Arañita only loses her train of thought three times and mentions that red isn't the right color for Santiago, my arm is sore from throwing the encyclopedia, and the longhorns at the agricultural center should really do a better job of keeping cadavers from wandering onto campus.

Profe puts his hands on his hips, taking in everything I've said. Captain Reynolds takes a deep breath and shakes his head. Pilar mumbles, "But he's not one of them."

We all stand around the DUD lying on the floor. No one says anything else. I have to bite my lip so Arañita doesn't fill the silence with noisy random thoughts.

Without responding to the mountain of information I just avalanched on him, Profe steps toward Santiago and looks him up and down.

"Are you okay, son?" he asks with a small smile.

Air rushes out of Santiago's lungs in relief and he nods. "Other than . . . being dead? . . . I think so."

Benji chuckles, and I elbow him in the ribs.

"Okay, well, first things first," Profe says to me. "Let's clean this up."

Profe slips on some gloves and hands me a pair. He crouches down at the DUD's head and slides his hands under the DUD's shoulders. He points his chin to the DUD's feet, and I wrap my hands around the cadaver's ankles. As we lift the DUD into the body bag, the skin on his right foot pulls and slides off in my hand like a loose sock.

"Nope. Not cool," Benji groans, looking away.

Captain Reynolds pivots on his heel and faces the library windows.

Taking an iPad out of his equipment pack, Profe kneels next to the DUD's right arm. The identification tag from the body farm is still attached to his wrist. The others must have fallen off as he wandered around campus.

As Profe examines the number on the tag, I stand next to him and whisper, "So you believe me? You're okay with Santiago?"

He looks up at me with a soft smile. "While I'm still trying to wrap my head around it scientifically, you know I'll always believe you, Frani."

My throat feels tight, and I think I might start crying right here. I wish I had told him what was going on a lot sooner, but I can see now that Arañita kept making up excuses not to.

After he zips up the body bag, Profe shows his iPad to Captain Reynolds.

"There's a bit of a problem," he says.

Captain Reynolds raises an eyebrow. "You mean other than this body wandering around campus and that one standing right there in front of me?"

Santiago gives Captain Reynolds a small wave, which makes Benji cackle, his voice echoing off the tile floor.

Profe nods. "This is Cadaver 082305. The one I reported missing to you was Cadaver 072201."

Captain Reynolds runs his hand over the stubble on his chin. "So there's still another one of these things . . . people out there?"

Benji looks at me and sighs. "More than one, sir. Frani tripped on another empty grave in the woods."

Captain Reynolds takes a deep breath. "Outstanding.

And I mean that in the most not outstanding way."

Pilar taps her foot on the tile floor, the sound echoing through the library.

"What was the cadaver number on the empty grave you found?" she asks me.

I close my eyes and try to picture the metal tag attached to the stake. But it's like Arañita has completely scrubbed the numbers from my mind. I can barely even imagine the grave. Plucking on other threads, she makes me begin to doubt that I even saw the hole in the ground or the cadaver numbers at all. I squeeze my hands into fists.

"I can't . . . ," I mutter, shaking my head.

"You don't . . . remember?" Santiago asks me.

My bottom lip quivers as I stomp my foot on the floor. "No."

Santiago shrugs slowly. "That's . . . okay. Me neither."

Profe slides his iPad back into his equipment pack and hands the bag to Benji. "No problem, Frani. We'll figure it out. Pilar and I will take this body back to the lab and see if we can't figure out what's going on. I'll have Dr. Tanaka do a scan of the entire facility to see if we're missing any more cadavers."

He stops for a moment when his breath hitches in his throat, as if he can't believe what he just said. He glances at Santiago before turning to Captain Reynolds.

"I'll keep you updated on what I find. Let me know if

there are any additional encounters on campus."

Captain Reynolds nods. "My officers don't carry guns. Will a Taser work to stop these things?"

"I recommend encyclopedias," I blurt out.

Captain Reynolds chuckles as Pilar helps Profe load the body bag onto the back of the side-by-side from the body farm. We hop in the seats behind Profe and Pilar, and speed away from the library as Captain Reynolds still shakes his head.

When we get back to the lab, Dr. Tanaka is waiting for us. I hope he's ready to meet Santiago. Profe didn't say a word the entire drive back to the lab, which I didn't really mind since Arañita was keeping me occupied with 462 scenarios of why the cadavers at the body farm are reanimating and it would've been difficult to focus on a conversation.

"You're okay?" Dr. Tanaka asks Benji immediately, wrapping him in a hug. He glances at Santiago, but luckily, it's now dark enough outside that he can't see Santiago's decomposed form.

"Cadaver 082305 was wandering around the library, and we still don't know where Cadaver 072201 is," I say, pointing my chin to the body bag in the back of the side-by-side. The sun has almost completely set behind the live oak trees. "And we have a new friend."

Santiago slowly gets out of the side-by-side and stands in front of Dr. Tanaka. The floodlight on the outside of the lab shines on Santiago, revealing every bit of loose skin, exposed muscle, and rotting flesh.

Dr. Tanaka draws in a sharp breath.

I quickly explain everything, a little better this time since I had a practice run when I told Profe and Captain Reynolds. Dr. Tanaka looks at Profe, who nods and says, "It's true. Not sure how, but it's true."

Dr. Tanaka slowly holds out a trembling hand for Santiago to shake.

Santiago smiles and waves his hand missing a finger. "Bad . . . idea."

Dr. Tanaka's eyes grow wide, and he looks at me and Benji. "You've had an adventure, haven't you?"

I nod. "And more adventures to come because we've got a lot to figure out."

Profe gets out of the side-by-side and puts his hands on his hips. "Dr. Tanaka, we'll need to scan the whole facility with the drone and do a walk-through to see if any more cadavers are missing. I hope it's only those two and the one Frani found in the woods."

Benji listens, but my gaze shifts down the hill. I squint my eyes in the growing dark, wondering how many empty holes we'll find. Arañita weaves a web of images and I don't hear what Profe, Pilar, and Dr. Tanaka are talking about. Hands pushing up through dirt. Snarling figures shuffling in the shadows.

"That's weird," Benji says, squeezing my hand and snapping me from my thoughts.

"What is?" I ask.

"Dad just said the body we brought back was an author."

I shrug. "So? Why is that weird? I mean, other than the fact that I have no idea how anyone concentrates long enough to write an entire book."

Dr. Tanaka helps Profe bring the body bag into the lab and set it on a table as we follow. Pilar slowly unzips the body bag while Profe and Dr. Tanaka continue talking.

"I just think it's interesting that this person was an author and we found them roaming outside the library," Benji says. "But I'm probably just letting my brain wander."

I chuckle. "I know what that's like."

Dr. Tanaka points to the DUD and Pilar steps back from it, lowering a pair of tweezers. "This is Mr. Zimmerman. I had to read his books in school, and I'll admit I didn't like them very much. It was a surprise when he showed up here as a donation."

Profe looks at Benji and me. "Y'all should head back up to the house. There's nothing we can do tonight to find the missing cadavers. It's too difficult in the dark. I'm going to try to figure out why this is happening."

"I can help," I say, planting my feet firmly on the ground.

Profe shakes his head. "I appreciate you wanting to help, but I think it's best if you rest now. It's been a busy day."

I don't know how to tell Profe that there's no way Arañita is going to let me get any sleep tonight.

"Pilar, do you have the beetle that Frani collected from Mr. Zimmerman?" Profe asks before we leave.

Pilar shakes her head. "I gave it to Frani. Right, Frani?"

"I . . . I don't think I have it," I stammer, closing my eyes and trying to remember the order of events in the library. Did Pilar give me the beetle? Arañita can't remember.

"We really need that bug," Profe says. "Are you sure you don't have it?"

My heart pounds in my ears in frustration. I shove my hands into my pockets, but the vial isn't there. I can't remember what happened to it after I slipped it into the brochure. It's like that memory was thrown out when I started imagining the possibly haunted third floor of the library.

"Excuse me . . . sir," Santiago says.

He shuffles slowly toward Profe. He reaches into the pocket of his pants. Holding out his four-fingered hand to Profe, he reveals a black beetle in the center of his palm.

"This is the same . . . bug as the one . . . Frani had," he says.

Profe takes the beetle from Santiago and slips it into a vial.

"Where did you get this?" Profe asks.

Santiago takes a deep breath. "It crawled . . . out of my ear."

"Awesome," Benji whispers.

Pilar's eyes grow wide. "How is that possible? You're not—"

She immediately stops and slaps her hand over her mouth. I narrow my eyes at Pilar.

I cross my arms and raise an eyebrow. "I think you know *exactly* how possible it is, Pilar," I say.

FIFTEEN

PILAR'S EYES GROW wide as her hand wraps around something in her pocket.

"What . . . what do you mean?" she asks, her voice shaking.

Her gaze drifts to the door, but Benji steps between her and possible escape.

I jut my chin to Pilar's hand in her pocket. Arañita lands on a thread and I clear my throat.

"If we looked in your pocket, the beetle would be in there, wouldn't it? Because I gave it to you. When I asked you about it, you tried to distract me by telling me the library was haunted. And now you're lying so that you can hide it!"

Pilar chuckles breathlessly, a forced sound that echoes in the lab as we all wait for her to respond. She shifts her weight from foot to foot.

"Wow, Frani Fran, that's quite a story," she says, blowing her hair off her forehead with a strained breath.

I shake my head and narrow my eyes. "Not a story. It happened."

Profe clears his throat and holds up the vial with the beetle that Santiago gave him. "Pilar, do you know anything about this? This beetle isn't typical of the types we find around or in decomposing cadavers. It's not a carrion beetle or a rove beetle. This is your specialty. Would you have any idea why we'd find something like this?"

Pilar bites her lip and scrunches her eyebrows together. "I . . . um . . ."

Dr. Tanaka sighs and puts his hands on his hips. "Show us what you have in your pocket."

Her breath quickening, Pilar opens her mouth to speak. But then she shakes her head and holds out her hand, revealing the vial I gave her. I stare at the skeleton tattoo on her arm as it quivers.

Santiago brushes against my bicep as he shuffles toward Pilar. He stares at her as he slowly lowers his gray hoodie, revealing the missing pieces of scalp, the split skin on his cheeks, and a lone maggot crawling out of his ear.

"What did . . . you do . . . to me?" he hisses as his chest heaves.

Pilar yelps and steps back. "But I didn't . . . but you're not . . . ," she stammers.

"Pilar!" Profe exclaims, and I jump. I've rarely heard

him raise his voice. He takes the vial from Pilar and compares it to the one from Santiago. They're the exact same bug. "Tell us what's going on right now."

With a heavy sigh, Pilar trudges over to the body bag on the table, giving Santiago lots of space, and unzips the bag as her fingers shake. She takes a deep breath and points to the left ear of the dead-again DUD.

Lifting a quivering finger to the vial in Profe's hand, Pilar mumbles, "That's a scarab beetle with an injection of electric eel DNA. I fed the beetles in through the ear canal so they could access the brain. I wanted to see if they would function like a defibrillator and restore brain function to cadavers. It was going to be groundbreaking research. No one had ever done it before."

Benji steps closer to me and whispers, "What's a defibrillator?"

"It's those electric paddle things that they use on people whose hearts have stopped beating. They shock their hearts back to beating again," I tell him.

Benji grunts. "She made one of those out of a bug?"

I raise my eyebrow. Even as randomly as Arañita seems to bounce from thread to thread, I don't think even she would land on doing something this extreme.

"You did what?" Dr. Tanaka exclaims, his eyes wide. "These people trust us with their bodies, Pilar. This violates all kinds of rules of ethics and science."

Pilar's lips purse in a tight line. "All we do every day is the same thing, over and over. Watching dead bodies slowly melt into the ground and turn into skeletons. It was time for something new. Science never advanced without taking risks," she mutters under her breath.

"What did you just say?" Profe barks. The veins in his forehead are throbbing.

Pilar slams her fist on the table. "I took a risk. A risk none of you were willing to take. Don't you ever want to find out what's possible? What could be?"

Profe shakes his head. "I want to help people! I want to respect their wishes. Their families trusted us. None of them agreed to this."

"Did that . . . happen to me?" Santiago whispers to me, not taking his gaze off the cadaver on the table.

I squeeze my eyes shut, imagining Santiago falling to the ground at the fence line between the agricultural center and the body farm. A lone brown beetle scurries across the rocks, over his hand lying on the ground, closer and closer to his ear. It tickles his cheek, scampering toward the dark space above his earlobe.

My eyes fly open. "This is the beetle you lost, isn't it? The one you asked us to help you find," I tell Pilar, pointing to the bug Santiago gave Profe. "You lost one of your Frankenbeetles, and it found its way to Santiago."

Pilar doesn't look at me but slowly nods her head.

Profe rubs his temples and takes a deep breath. "How many? How many cadavers did you do this to?"

Pilar crosses her arms, the skeleton on her bicep stretching and looking like it's screaming. Gone is the person who used to make jokes about changing the name of the facility or playing rock paper scissors with Dr. Tanaka. She's a completely different Pilar, a hard, determined look on her face.

"Five," she says, lifting her chin almost with pride.

My eyebrows rise. We found Mr. Zimmerman, the library DUD, but that means there's still the one from the empty grave in the woods, plus three more wandering around somewhere out there. Not to mention Santiago.

"And what about my friend?!" I blurt out. "He didn't do anything to you, and you infected him. Did you kill him first just so you could do your stupid experiment?"

"Frani," Benji says, pulling on my arm. I shake him off as heat rises to my cheeks and my eyes burn.

Pilar gasps and shakes her head furiously, staring at Santiago. "I . . . I'd never do anything like that."

"Oh, really?" My voice echoes in the lab. Arañita turns up the volume and I don't care. "Sounds to me like you're willing to do anything. Even if it means hurting people. People who just wanted to be left alone!"

"No, that's not it. I mean, look what our amazing brains can do! Only people like us can think so far outside the box, Frani Fran—"

"Don't call me that!" I scream. Hot tears pool in my eyes. "You're a terrible person. I hate you!"

Pilar opens her mouth to speak. She looks from me to Profe and Dr. Tanaka. Her breath hitches in her throat.

She takes one last look at Santiago and turns to dart toward the door. But Santiago reaches out, grabbing her forearm. She jerks and I hear a snap as Santiago's hand dislocates from his wrist and hangs loose. Dr. Tanaka steps in front of Pilar.

"You're not going anywhere. You need to be held responsible for what you've done," he says.

I double over and put my hands on my knees, my chest heaving. I can't seem to slow my breath down no matter how much I try to concentrate.

Profe sinks onto a stool and sighs. He rubs a hand along his chin and stares at the cadaver in front of him. He takes his phone out of his pocket and dials.

"Captain Reynolds," he says when it connects. "I've got someone in my lab who needs to be taken into custody. They're the reason this whole mess is happening. Please send an officer as soon as possible."

Profe hangs up and looks at Pilar. He shakes his head and rubs his hand on his chin.

Dr. Tanaka stands next to Pilar as she sits on a stool, his hand firmly on her shoulder. "Now what, Profe?" he asks.

Profe thinks for a moment. I watch him, wondering if

he's thinking of a list of things to do in the exact order we should do them. Arañita is flying from picturing Pilar out in the field, pushing beetles into cadavers' ears, to Santiago wandering around alone, to faceless bodies shuffling in the dark across campus. I can't get her to land on a single thought and stick with it.

I shake my head and grunt.

"You okay, Frani?" Benji asks.

My chin quivers. Today has been too much.

"We've got a lot to do. I want to examine these beetles and figure out exactly what she did and which cadavers she did it to," Profe says, pointing at Pilar. "Unless she wants to give us all the details now."

Pilar crosses her arms and grunts, her lips in a tight line.

"So, you infected five cadavers. We know of one," Dr. Tanaka says to her, nodding at the cadaver on the table.

"It's actually two, Dad," Benji says, standing next to Santiago and helping him cover his head with his hoodie again.

Dr. Tanaka turns to us. "What?"

Benji clears his throat. "Captain Reynolds told us about a woman in a Pikachu onesie who wandered onto the football field. I think that might be one of the cadavers in your experiment."

Profe nods. "Well, I guess it's on us to figure out exactly who the other three are. But we can't do that in the dark.

The best thing we can do is get some rest. Tomorrow is going to be a long day."

Benji grabs my hand. "C'mon, Frani. Let's go home."

I shake my head and look at Santiago. He's cradling his limp left hand in his right arm. "But what about Santiago?" I ask. "We have to figure out how to help him."

Profe gets up from his stool and puts his hand on my shoulder. "Rest, Frani. Sometimes it's the most productive thing you can do."

I scoff. That's easy for him to say. Arañita never lets me rest. And I'm just starting to realize how tired I am.

SIXTEEN

BENJI SPENDS THE night curled up on our couch, wrapped like a burrito in three blankets. He told his mom we were having a *One Piece* anime marathon.

"Dad said that was better than telling her it's more like a 'Multiple Undead Pieces' marathon," he says, yawning wide as he pulls my fuzzy brown-and-white blanket with a huge lion on it over his shoulder.

I roll my eyes.

"Too soon?" he says with a wink.

Santiago grunts from Profe's recliner, which he's sitting in. He pulls up Essie's purple floral blanket that she doesn't know I've borrowed yet because she's thankfully staying at Yaikira's house tonight. She won't be home to witness the decomposing body under her blanket.

"So, do you sleep?" I ask, handing Santiago another pillow.

He thinks a moment and then shrugs. "Don't know. . . . Haven't tried yet."

Benji rolls over on his side and faces Santiago. "But are you still hungry?"

"A little," Santiago says, taking a deep breath. "Your fingers look like . . . chicken tenders."

Benji looks at me and raises an eyebrow.

"Kidding." Santiago chuckles.

I rub my temples, torn between wanting to help Santiago and being curled up in my bed. I know Arañita won't let me sleep at all tonight.

When I head to my bedroom, I decide to scroll through Story Stack after Arañita makes up five stories about how Santiago could've ended up at the body farm, each one worse than the last. There aren't any new comments on my post about him.

When Arañita finally can't fight against my growing exhaustion and calms down on her web, I dream of a red-hooded figure, scuffing their feet in the dirt as beetles the size of small cars chase after him.

I don't sleep well.

The next morning, Benji is already waiting at my bedroom door when I wake up.

"We've got a problem," he says, his black hair sticking out in every direction.

"Another one for the long list of problems we already have?" I ask, groaning as I stretch.

Benji leads me out into the living room, where Santiago

is still sitting in Profe's recliner.

"He took his shoes off. And, um, his toes too," Benji says, pointing to Santiago's feet.

I look at the beige living room carpet and spot four gray toes.

"Sorry," Santiago says, slipping his feet back into his worn-out Vans. "I think I'm two . . . shoe sizes smaller now."

"It's not your fault," I say.

"We need to come up with something to slow this down," Benji says.

Arañita goes flying as I picture Santiago in the freezer in the lab and think of the first time I saw snow in Colorado, which makes me think of the really tasty elk burger I ate there, which makes me wonder how much elk weigh.

Arañita is no help.

"I need . . . cold," Santiago says, slowly standing from the recliner. We wrapped his wrist tightly with a bandage last night to keep the disconnected bones from dangling.

Hurrying over to the fridge in the kitchen, Benji opens the freezer. "I've got it," he says.

When he comes back over to us, he has four ice packs in his hands. We tuck two into Santiago's shirt and the other two in the pockets of his jeans.

"What about the other thing?" Benji asks.

"What other thing?" I raise my eyebrow.

Santiago takes a deep breath. "Still . . . hungry. Benji

looks like . . . a Whataburger meal."

"If you promise not to snack on me, I'll give you canned chicken soup, spaghetti, or grilled cheese," Benji says, stepping away from Santiago. "Those are the only things I know how to make. Do any of those sound good?"

Santiago slowly shakes his head.

"Then with whatever electrical impulses you have left in your brain, don't think about eating. Anything," I tell him.

After I change and Benji eats four Pop-Tarts, we head out to the lab. When we get there, Profe is hunched over a rectangular metal tray where two beetles lie lifeless, each secured to a foam block with small pins.

Our library DUD, Mr. Zimmerman, is free of his body bag and stretched out on the table. A straight line across his forehead reveals where Profe cut through his skull with a small circular saw to examine his brain. The DUD's brain is on a tray next to his head, cut into thin slices like a loaf of bread. I know this lets Profe examine each part of his brain to see exactly how Pilar's beetles affected it.

"First Rice Krispies, now sandwiches. I'm never going to eat again," Benji groans.

I come up behind Profe and wrap my arms around him. "Good morning," I tell him. "What time did you get up?"

He pats my arm and sighs, nudging my cheek with his temple. "I had a very early call from the university president about the mess at the library. Captain Reynolds and I have to get our stories straight until we figure everything out."

Benji smiles. "Well, sir. The DUD Search and Rescue Team is reporting for duty."

Raising an eyebrow, Profe asks, "DUD?"

"Definitely Undead Dude, sir," Benji answers.

I turn to Profe. "So what did you find out?"

He points to the DUD's brain on the table with his scalpel. "Well, Pilar really did do what she said she did. If it wasn't so unethical, it would be fascinating. The beetles burrowed deep into the brain and caused electrical charges throughout the matter. This managed to reanimate the corpses. But simply having basic brain activity again didn't exactly bring them back to life. They're still a shell of their former selves."

I think for a moment. "But if Santiago was infected by the same beetle, why is he so different? He can talk and he isn't trying to snack on our livers."

"Yet," Benji says, and Santiago winks at him.

Profe examines Santiago. "Since you weren't part of her experiment, something else must've happened to you to enhance the effects of Pilar's experiment."

"Lightning? Toxic waste? A ghost?" I ask as Arañita bounces over Benji's previous theories.

Profe shakes his head with a chuckle. "One of Captain Reynolds's officers picked up Pilar. They're going to hold her at the university station until we can figure out what to tell the San Zavala Police Department. There are certain things I think we should leave out."

Benji drums his fingers on his thigh, thinking. He points to Mr. Zimmerman on the table. "So, my dad said this DUD was an author? And we found him wandering around a library. The more I think about it, the more it seems like those two things are connected."

Arañita starts plucking at three different strings, but it's still too confusing for me to put my thoughts together in actual sentences.

Profe looks at Benji. "Are you hypothesizing that these reanimated corpses are drawn to whatever they were connected to in their former lives?"

Benji nods slowly. "I think so, but you said it in way fancier words."

"Math building," I blurt out.

Profe and Benji look at me.

"Give us more, Frani," Profe says. The soft smile on his face lets me know that he's encouraging me and not judging me.

"We found Santiago sitting outside the math building on campus. He can do calculations really quickly, even with a decomposing brain. And it was Santiago's math teacher who reported him missing."

Santiago purses his lips. "I don't know . . . why I went there. It just . . . felt right."

Profe sets his scalpel down. He pushes the tray of beetles away. "I think you kids are onto something. But let's take care of first things first. I need you to go out with Dr. Tanaka and determine exactly which cadavers Pilar infected. But if your hypothesis is correct, we can look up information about the cadavers and what their lives were like. That may help us narrow down where they have wandered."

Profe stops himself and swallows hard. "I don't think I'm going to get used to saying things like this."

Benji and I head out the far lab door and into the field. Santiago stays with Profe in the cool lab since that's better for his decomposition than wandering around in the Texas heat. Dr. Tanaka is waiting for us, a drone case at his feet.

Over the next couple of hours, Benji controls the drone, scanning the entire facility, searching for burial plots empty of their residents. Benji tells us over the radio the sections he thinks may be empty, and Dr. Tanaka and I head out there in a side-by-side. We find that in addition to Mr. Zimmerman and Cadaver 122305, who ends up being Ms. Gloriana Soto, we're also missing Cadavers 072201, 072405 and 062405. That makes the five Pilar says she infected with beetles.

I get the cadaver numbers wrong three times, though, because Essie keeps texting me complaining about not taking out the trash and how she can't find her purple blanket. Dr. Tanaka has to check what I've written down in my notebook each time, and I hate that he probably thinks I'm not good at what I'm doing because Arañita won't focus.

Dr. Tanaka speeds the side-by-side back to the lab so we can look up information about each cadaver. When we screech to a stop, dust flying in the air, Benji is packing up the drone.

"Only thing worse than looking for missing cadavers is finding a nest of baby rattlesnakes in the process," Dr. Tanaka says, hopping out of the side-by-side.

"Really, Dad?" Benji smirks. "I'm pretty sure DUDs wandering around is always gonna top the list."

"No, your dad's right," I say, wiping the sweat off my forehead. "We found a bunch of rattlesnakes down by the fence. One bite and you get to be a resident at the body farm."

"Let's get that list to Profe," Dr. Tanaka says, patting me on the back. "You've got it, Frani?"

I hop out of the side-by-side. "Yep."

And then I look next to my seat. The notebook where I was writing down the cadavers' numbers isn't there. I check the back of the side-by-side. No notebook.

"Do you have the list?" I ask Dr. Tanaka. My voice shakes as I try to remember the last time I had it. But Arañita cut that thread. No matter how hard I squeeze my eyes shut and try to picture step-by-step what Dr. Tanaka and I did out in the field, I can't.

I glance at Benji. He has his hands on his hips and he's blowing his bangs off his forehead with a long sigh. He probably thinks I'm an idiot for not being able to do the simplest thing. I've been waiting for the one thing that will make him realize that Arañita is too weird, too much for us to be friends, and this is probably it. My stomach flip-flops, and I try to swallow the lump in my throat.

Dr. Tanaka shakes his head. "I'm sure we just left it at our last stop. Don't worry, Frani. We'll find it. It's okay."

"It's not okay!" I blurt out. "This is important, and I can't even keep track of a stupid little notebook."

I stomp my feet in the dirt, heat rising to my cheeks. Arañita flies over her web. She tells me it was easy for Pilar to distract me in the library so she could pocket her beetle. That making me think I never gave the beetle to Profe in the first place was simple because I can't remember anything properly.

Arañita doesn't let me forget that I'm useless.

Benji hops into the back of the side-by-side. "Let's go get your notebook, Frani," he says, patting the seat in front of him.

I slide into the seat but clench my fists, still trying to remember the last time I had the notebook. Arañita plucks on a thread of me eating a Pop-Tart this morning, then bounces to me standing over an empty plot of dirt as Dr. Tanaka reads the cadaver number from the stake at the edge. But no matter how much I concentrate, I can't picture the last time I had the notebook.

I'm so frustrated, I want to scream. I don't even hear the conversation Dr. Tanaka and Benji are having.

Dr. Tanaka stops the side-by-side in front of the last burial site we visited. I look and see the green notebook sitting right on top of a rock, the cover blowing open in the breeze and flipping the pages.

I run over and grab it. Even now, holding it in my hands, I can't remember leaving it here. Tears spill over and fall down my cheeks. I sit down in the dirt and hold the notebook to my chest.

Benji comes up to me and puts his hand on my shoulder. His hand is hot on my skin and I hate the feeling of his touch. "It's okay, Frani," he says. "See? We found it."

I rock back and forth. "No, it's not okay! I'm useless. I can't even do the simplest things."

I hate Arañita.

I hate my brain.

I hate myself.

SEVENTEEN

I DON'T SAY anything when I hand the notebook to Profe in the lab. I slump down on a stool as he looks over the list. He types the cadaver numbers into his iPad and pulls up their information.

Dr. Tanaka, Profe, and Benji talk as Profe scrolls through his files, but I'm hardly listening. I pick at the cuticle on my thumb because the fact that it's loose from my nail is all Arañita lets me think about.

I'm certain they feel I'm overreacting. That it's silly to get so upset over misplacing a notebook. But this sort of thing happens all the time. I can't trust my own brain because Arañita is always sabotaging it.

"Are you . . . okay?" Santiago asks. He reaches out for my hand but stops himself.

"I'm tired of being different," I tell him.

Santiago smiles and points to the long cut on his cheek with a nail-less finger. "Me too."

I shake my head. "It's not the same. My brain is just too weird."

Nudging me with his sharp elbow, Santiago chuckles. "I think I win . . . the weird brain prize . . . no contest."

Benji glances in my direction and shuffles over. He looks at my now-bleeding thumb.

"Did I ever tell you about the time I lost Dad's car keys and he found them three hours later on top of chicken in the freezer after he was super late for work?" he says.

I sigh. "You don't have to try to make me feel better. It won't work."

"I'm not trying to make you feel better. I'm letting you know we all make mistakes and get frustrated," he says, shrugging.

I glare at him. "I'm pretty sure no one here has made as many stupid mistakes as I do."

"I somehow . . . ended up on a farm . . . with dead bodies. And then . . . became a DUD," Santiago says. He tries to wink at me, but his eyelids stick together.

Dr. Tanaka's laughter echoes in the lab. "You really haven't been paying attention, Frani. Have you ever injected cadavers with genetically modified beetles, causing the bodies to come back to life and wreak havoc on an entire university? Because I think that's currently in the running for the worst mistake."

I can't help but chuckle as I wipe tears from my cheeks. Profe walks over to me and wraps me in a hug. "I love you and I love your brain," he whispers in my ear.

I want to cry all over again.

"You know what else I'd love?" Profe asks, holding my chin in his hands and lifting my head. "I'd love your help with this because we're stuck, and we need someone who thinks outside the box."

I smile. "Even if it's highly possible that I'll lose the box?"

Dr. Tanaka and Benji laugh as Profe leads me over to the table where his iPad rests.

He walks me through the information about the missing cadavers. As I scan each of their names, one pops out, and Arañita starts plucking hard at a thread.

"The football team!" I exclaim.

"Walk us back a little, Frani," Profe says.

I take a deep breath, trying to retrace why that popped out of my mouth.

"Ms. Soto is one of the missing cadavers. It says in her information that she was a bodybuilder. Don't you think someone like that would be likely to challenge an entire football team to prove how strong she is? She was dressed in a Pikachu onesie. Is that what you put Ms. Soto in for your experiment, Dr. Tanaka?"

I feel out of breath after I finish speaking. I glance from

Santiago, Dr. Tanaka, and Benji to Profe as they take in what I've said.

Dr. Tanaka nods. "Yep. That's her. I was testing fire-resistant material."

Benji takes the notebook from Profe and writes down *Ms. Soto—gyms, athletic fields*.

"Who else?" I ask.

Profe scrolls the screen on his iPad. "One of them is pretty recent—Mr. Gearhart."

I bite my lip and think. "Cars. Anywhere with cars, maybe," I say.

"He was the mechanic, wasn't he?" Dr. Tanaka asks.

I nod. Benji writes Mr. Gearhart's name in the notebook and then puts *cars* after it.

"That's a little too general, though," Profe says. "There are cars everywhere."

Putting my hands on my hips, I close my eyes and think of the story I wrote about Mr. Gearhart. I imagined how much he loved Patsy and how they would go cruising every Sunday in an old car he'd fixed up. "Car shows, mechanic shops, anywhere there are classic cars. I think maybe that's what he'd be drawn to," I say.

Benji edits Mr. Gearhart's clues in the notebook. We go through the other two cadavers, Mr. Hutchinson and Ms. Prado, and brainstorm what they might possibly be attracted to as DUDs based on their biographical information.

"Now what?" I ask. "Do we just wander around these places, hoping we run into a DUD?"

Profe takes out his cell phone. "First, I'm going to fill Captain Reynolds in on everything we've figured out."

"Like spies," I blurt out.

"More?" Profe says.

"We need to be as undercover and quick as possible. Like spies. Because student orientation is coming up and there's going to be way more people on campus. And you probably don't want any more calls from the university."

Profe groans as he dials a number on his phone and steps away from us. As he talks to Captain Reynolds, Dr. Tanaka takes the notebook from Benji. "Where do we start?" he asks.

"I want . . . to help," Santiago says.

Dr. Tanaka raises an eyebrow. "Is that going to be safe?"

"We put ice packs in Santiago's clothes to keep him cool and slow down his decomposition," I say.

But when I look at Santiago, there's a large wet spot on his shirt where the ice packs have melted.

"Those will probably need to be replaced," Benji says.

"So fresh ice packs. Got it," Dr. Tanaka says, and then shakes his head. Everyone is still getting used to a DUD being a regular part of their day, I think.

When Profe gets off the phone, he comes back over to us. "I'm assuming we have a plan?" he asks.

"We have a suggestion of a plan. A whiff of a plan. An aftertaste of a plan," Benji says.

I roll my eyes. "Don't worry, Profe. We've got it. We know the most likely places for these DUDs to show up. But I guess the bigger question is, what do we do if we find them? I don't think we can throw encyclopedias at all of them."

Benji's eyes light up. "Oh! This is it. My time has come," he says.

"What are you talking about?" Dr. Tanaka asks, raising his eyebrow at his son.

"I've been preparing for this my whole life," Benji responds.

"All twelve years?" I blurt out.

Benji ignores me. "Do you know how many hours of anime and horror movies I've watched? How many manga I've read that have prepared me for this exact moment? I know exactly what to do."

"So, what do we need to do?" Profe asks.

Benji puffs up his chest. "It's the brain. It's always the brain. We have to destroy it. That's why Frani and I were able to stop the DUD in the library. He cracked his head on the floor after she pummeled him with a book."

Santiago stares at the ground and shoves his hands

into the pockets of his hoodie as Benji makes wild gestures showing how we defeated Mr. Zimmerman.

"Well, Benji," Profe says. "I hate to burst your bubble, but I would like to do everything we can to try to limit damage to these cadavers. It's always our mission to be as respectful as possible with those who've been entrusted into our care."

Dr. Tanaka nods. "Even though Pilar pretty much ignored that."

Profe's eyebrows knit together as he thinks. "I don't want to hit them over the head with anything, books or otherwise. I don't want to stab their brains or chop their heads off, no matter how many horror movies you've seen," he says, looking at Benji.

"That . . . sounds good," Santiago says.

Benji's shoulders sag. "So, what do we do?"

Arañita hops around and I squeeze my eyes shut, holding on while she drags me across fifteen separate thoughts. It's like she's electrified, and for a moment, one of the threads she jumps on wonders if I've been infected by Pilar's beetles too.

"Chocolate cake is my favorite birthday cake flavor," I finally say.

"I agree," Benji says, unfazed. "But it's too soft to throw at DUDs."

"True. But last year for my birthday, Essie made me a three-layer chocolate cake and got mad that Profe and I wouldn't come back to the house and eat it because we were walking through the body farm, documenting if any of the cadavers had been affected by wildlife. Profe had a tranquilizer gun just in case we had to deal with any coyotes. It's the one we use in case any of the animals from the agricultural center wander onto the property."

Profe claps his hands together, a big smile on his face. "That's it. That's what we'll use."

Dr. Tanaka nods. "That'll be perfect to slow down and stop the cadavers so we can bring them back to the lab. But since it's safe to assume they don't have blood flow any longer, we have to make sure we hit them with the tranquilizer directly in the temple, the ear, or the base of the neck. Otherwise, the tranquilizer won't get to their brain."

Profe heads to the far corner of the lab and removes a metal case from a shelf. Opening it, he takes out two guns that look like pistols and hands one to Dr. Tanaka. He also hands Dr. Tanaka a clear case that has four darts with bright pink puffs on one end. When they come back over to us, Benji holds his hand out.

"I've always wanted to shoot one of those!"

Dr. Tanaka shakes his head. "Not in a million years, son. But we still need a permanent solution. Because tranquilizers wear off."

Santiago glances at me, and I give him a half-hearted thumbs-up.

Benji groans.

"All right, let's head out. We'll take the side-by-side onto campus. We'll go through the list you've got for each DUD and hope we come across them," Profe says. "If we do, Dr. Tanaka and I will neutralize them with the tranquilizer guns and then load them in body bags to bring back here to the lab."

"Oh, maggot nostrils, we're lucky it's Saturday. There won't be many students on campus to freak out about us riding around, shooting darts at the undead," I say.

Profe rubs his temples. "I'm really not looking forward to the meeting with the university president that I will most definitely have about this, but I'll worry about that later."

Benji looks at each of us and shoots his hand out. "All right, team!"

I reach out and put my hand on top of his. Santiago gently places his hand with the missing pinky finger on top of mine. Dr. Tanaka smirks and places his hand on top of Santiago's, and Profe lays his hand on top of Dr. Tanaka's.

"Show no mercy to the undead. Protect the living. Prepare for battle!" Benji shrieks.

Profe clears his throat. "How about 'Respect the dead. Protect the living. Do no harm,'" he says.

Benji groans. "You're kind of ruining this for me, sir."

“Go, DUD Search and Rescue Team!” I shout with a laugh.

We cheer and push our hands down, heading out to round up any shuffling figure without a pulse wandering around campus.

EIGHTEEN

AS WE RIDE through the agricultural center, I look at Santiago.

"You doing okay with all of this?" I ask him.

He shrugs and I hear his shoulder joint pop. "Is it bad to say . . . this is really fun? I don't think I was ever . . . part of a team . . . when I was alive. At least . . . it doesn't feel like I was."

I glance at everyone in the side-by-side. "We've got a pretty good team here. And we've got your back."

"Literally?" Santiago smirks.

I nudge him. "You know what I mean."

We replaced the ice packs in Santiago's clothes, and I wonder how long they'll last as we drive outside under the strong sun.

Dr. Tanaka speeds past a herd of Black Angus cows and through the gate to campus as Benji, Santiago, and I are pressed together in the back seat of the side-by-side. We try to look as casual as possible driving past students with a decomposing friend sitting between Benji and me. All the *Welcome Back* signs hanging from practically every building remind us that we need to round up these DUDs soon.

"Oh no!" I gasp as Arañita plucks on a thread. "Mr. Hutchinson!"

"What about him?" Benji asks as Dr. Tanaka drives past the library.

"He led fishing charters on the Gulf Coast, right?" I say.

Profe nods. "That's what his file said."

"Well, I was just thinking if he's attracted to water, he might be down by the river. And that's where all the students tend to hang out on the weekends. They'll see him!"

"Hope he looks . . . better than I do," Santiago says, taking a face mask out of his pocket and slipping it on.

Dr. Tanaka grips the steering wheel. "We'll deal with that when it comes to it. Right now, I was thinking we should head to the football stadium since that's the only place we've had an actual cadaver sighting. There's a definite chance Ms. Soto is still around there."

"Dad! Stop!" Benji shouts, and I grip Profe's seat in front of me as Dr. Tanaka slams on the brakes.

"What is it?" Dr. Tanaka asks.

"Look," Benji says, lifting a finger and pointing to the large parking lot behind the student center.

It's filled with classic cars of every color. Old men sit in lawn chairs next to the cars and chat while others walk around, admiring the red Mustangs and blue Corvettes.

"Mr. Gearhart?" I ask Benji.

He nods. "It's as good a chance as any, right?"

Dr. Tanaka maneuvers the side-by-side to the edge of the parking lot. He and Profe put their tranquilizer guns in backpacks and Dr. Tanaka hands Santiago a pair of sunglasses.

"There's a chance your eyes look like they're made of fire ants. Best put those on," he says.

Santiago slips on the sunglasses and we walk around the car show. I get distracted looking at an old dark green Ford truck with wood paneling on the bed since it's exactly like a toy truck I used to play with when I was little.

I tell Benji and he says, "Don't forget we're supposed to be looking for Mr. Gearhart."

Waving my hand at the parking lot, I say, "He's gonna be a dead guy shuffling around in a purple sweatsuit. I think we'll hear screams and shouts before we see him."

After going up and down each row of the car show, making sure Mr. Gearhart somehow wasn't hiding in the back seat of any of the vehicles, Dr. Tanaka and Profe come up to Santiago, Benji, and me.

"He's not here," Dr. Tanaka says.

Benji nods. "Yeah, I think we can check this place off our list."

I look around the parking lot and across the street. The

road borders the edge of campus and there's a mechanic's shop on the other side. "How about over there?"

Profe shrugs. "Doesn't hurt to check, I guess."

We head across the street to Rodriguez's Llantas y Mecanica. The three cars parked in front of the building look like they're held together with more duct tape than actual car parts.

We scan up and down the front of the building, but there's no sign of Mr. Gearhart. Profe and Dr. Tanaka head into the work bay, where a black SUV is held up by a large yellow lift. A man in a dark blue button-down shirt comes out, wiping his hands on a rag that seems as dirty as his hands are.

"Can I help y'all with something?" he asks, streaks of black grease on his forearms.

"I hope so," Profe says. "We're from the university. We're looking for someone. Have you seen a man wandering around here in a purple sweatsuit? He'd definitely look out of place."

The man in the blue shirt shrugs. "I suppose the only folks around here that look out of place are you five."

Profe chuckles. "Yeah, I guess you're right. Would you mind if I gave you my card so you could contact me in case you do see something?"

The man nods and takes the card Profe hands him from his pocket. "This isn't about those football players getting attacked, is it? Buddy of mine swears the university is making superhuman mutants. Y'all's experiments get out of control or something?"

Profe laughs again, but it obviously sounds more forced this time. "Oh, no. It's nothing like that. Thanks for your time."

We head back across the street with the mechanic shouting after us, "I'll be sure to call you if I see your mutant!"

Santiago nudges me with his elbow. "I'm not . . . a mutant. Am I?"

I shrug. "You're an interesting scientific specimen. But you're our friend too."

As we load into the side-by-side, I brush off light pink petals that blew in from the tree we parked under and onto my seat.

"Flowers!" I say.

"Excellent work identifying the local plants, Frani. You're right," Benji says with a wink.

I punch him on the arm. "No, you maggot nostril. Mr. Gearhart's tattoo."

"The heart with the name Patsy in it?" Dr. Tanaka asks.

I nod. "Yeah, but do you remember what was around the heart? It was flowers."

"You wouldn't happen to remember what kind of flowers, would you?" Profe asks, lowering his backpack from his shoulder and taking out the tranquilizer gun.

I look around. A smile grows on my face when I see what I'm looking for.

"They were flowers just like those down the hill," I say, pointing past the student center to a small, steep hill where trees grow right on the bank of the river. At the base of one of the trees is a patch of bright yellow daffodils.

And next to the daffodils is Mr. Gearhart.

I chuckle. "It wasn't cars that he was drawn to. It was Patsy. It's always been Patsy."

"There he is!" Benji says.

Dr. Tanaka takes his tranquilizer gun out of his backpack. "You three stay up here. Profe and I will neutralize him and then you bring down a body bag so we can load him up."

Santiago reaches out a hand and places it on Dr. Tanaka's shoulder.

"Can I . . . try something first?" he asks. "Maybe we have . . . a connection. Since we're . . . both dead."

Dr. Tanaka looks at Profe, who nods. "Can't resist a scientific experiment," Profe says.

Santiago takes off his sunglasses and slips them into the pocket of his hoodie. He slowly walks down the hill toward Mr. Gearhart.

I watch as Mr. Gearhart stares at the daffodils at his feet. He'd only been buried in the field two days before Pilar's beetle made him come back from the dead, so the decomposition on his body isn't too severe. His eyes are rimmed red, and I can see from the sweatshirt pulled up his back that his skin still has a deep purple color from where his blood settled in livor mortis.

He reaches an arm out slowly toward the daffodils and his back jerks back and forth, as if he's trying to bend down and pick the flowers, but his muscles are too tight. I watch his mouth open and close, his lips coming together like he's trying to blow out birthday candles.

It's like he's trying to say a word. Maybe *Patsy*.

Reaching Mr. Gearhart, Santiago bends down with a grunt, his tense muscles straining. He plucks a daffodil from the ground and holds it out to Mr. Gearhart.

For a moment, I think that Mr. Gearhart is remembering Patsy, remembering what it felt like when he was alive. He stares at the flower for several moments as Santiago begins to smile.

But then Mr. Gearhart stumbles forward and gnashes his teeth. He swings his arm at Santiago and the daffodil falls to the ground.

"Abort mission, Dad," Benji says. "It's tranquilizer time."

I grip a thick body bag in my hand as Dr. Tanaka and Profe walk down the hill toward Mr. Gearhart. The area is overgrown with trees, so luckily no one on campus is about to see two men approach a guy and shoot him in the forehead with a dart.

Because that's exactly what happens.

When the dart hits Mr. Gearhart, he grunts and his eyes grow wide. Looking at Profe and Dr. Tanaka, he takes three shuffling steps forward and then falls to the ground. Dr. Tanaka walks over to him and nudges Mr. Gearhart's torso with his boot. When Mr. Gearhart doesn't respond, Dr. Tanaka waves Benji and me over with the body bag.

We scurry down the hill and lay out the bag next to Mr. Gearhart.

"I thought . . . I could help him," Santiago says, scuffing his feet on the ground.

I gently pat him on the back as Dr. Tanaka and Profe carefully load Mr. Gearhart's body into the bag.

Santiago looks at me. He starts to bite his lip but stops. "Why am I . . . so different?"

I reach into Santiago's pocket and take out his sunglasses, holding them out. "I ask that about myself every day," I tell him.

It takes all four of us to carry the body bag up the hill as Santiago follows us, and I'm quickly out of breath. We put the bag in the back of the side-by-side with a grunt.

"Well, that's two down, four to go, right?" Benji asks.

I nod. "Yep. We still have Ms. Soto, Mr. Hutchinson, Ms. Prado, and Santiago."

"Yeah, but this one was easy. I bet the rest will be just

like it," Dr. Tanaka says.

Benji and I look at him, our mouths dropped open.

"What?" Profe asks. "What'd he say?"

"Oh, maggot nostrils," I mumble.

Benji nods. "Dad, you can't say stuff like that. Once my teacher said she was having a really chill day and then her computer shot sparks out of the keyboard, the kid next to me threw up, and the fire alarms went off."

"Sentences like that are off-limits," I groan. "We're really gonna be in for it now."

We get back in the side-by-side. "Well, we only have a few more hours left of daylight for things to be as horrible as you expect," Profe says. "Let's head over to the football stadium like we planned."

As much as I try to stop her, Arañita spends the whole ride there plucking strings that toss images of Ms. Soto lifting me above her head with an ear-bursting scream and throwing me into a stack of weights in the football team's weight room.

This is gonna be rough.

NINETEEN

WHEN DR. TANAKA stops the side-by-side in front of the football stadium, the sun sits lower on the horizon, the sky turning a deep orange. The large bobcat logo for Central Texas University looks more maroon than red in the fading light.

"We don't have much longer today. Let's hope Ms. Soto is around here," Profe says, scanning up and down the walkways in front of the stadium.

"She's definitely here," a voice calls to us.

I look at the bottom of the stairs leading into the stadium and see Captain Reynolds.

"Did you get my message?" he asks Profe when we walk up to him.

Profe shakes his head and pulls his phone out of his back pocket. "Sorry, we've been a little preoccupied with the current situation."

Captain Reynolds nods. "Understandable. You find one of them?" he asks, pointing to Mr. Gearhart's body bag on the back of the side-by-side.

"Yeah, he was down by the narrow part of the riverbank near the student center. Looking at some flowers, of all things," Dr. Tanaka explains. "We neutralized him with a tranquilizer gun."

"Good idea," Captain Reynolds says.

"It was Frani's idea," Benji says, nudging me. "Frani remembered these flowers he had tattooed on his arm around his wife's name, and we saw those same flowers by the river."

"You still doing okay, son?" Captain Reynolds asks Santiago, looking him up and down.

Santiago lowers his hoodie, but the fabric sticks to his skin and pulls off his right ear. It falls to the sidewalk and rolls to Captain Reynolds's feet.

"Does that answer your question?" I say as Santiago shuffles over to his ear, picks it up, and slips it into the pocket of his hoodie. I'm beginning to wonder how many spare body parts he has in there.

Captain Reynolds shakes his head and waves us toward the entrance of the stadium. "We got another call of someone wandering around here. I figured it was our . . . um, a not-alive individual."

"She wasn't in the weight room, was she?" I ask, my voice quivering slightly. Arañita is still hyperfocused on me getting destroyed under a mountain of dumbbells and weight plates.

Captain Reynolds chuckles. "No, she's out on the field. We cleared the area. The football coach isn't so mad at me anymore. I think he's about to recruit this woman for a defensive lineman position."

I raise my eyebrows. "Does he know she's dead?"

Captain Reynolds shakes his head. "I didn't have the heart to explain that part. I can hardly believe it myself. But look," he says, gesturing to the football field.

In the center of the grass is a tackling dummy, a tall, padded post sticking up from two skis on the ground that let the dummy slide backward when a player crashes into it.

Except it's not a football player currently launching themselves into the dummy.

It's Ms. Soto.

She's wearing the Pikachu onesie that Dr. Tanaka put her in to study the effects of fire-resistant fabric on decomposition. Her hair mat has slipped off, her bare skull looking like a football helmet on her head. The artificial turf on the field is rough on her feet and her skin has worn away from her heels and toes. Each time she slams into the tackling dummy with a loud grunt, I'm certain the skin on her shoulders and torso is pulling and splitting. We have to stop her before she hurts herself too much.

"She seems . . . strong," Captain Reynolds says.

Profe nods, loading another dart into his tranquilizer gun. "She looks like she could fling any of us straight through the goalposts."

I chuckle nervously. "For sure. We're in trouble with this one."

"Because *somebody* said these were all going to be easy." Benji sighs, turning to his dad and raising his eyebrow.

Dr. Tanaka lifts his hands in surrender. "Sorry."

Clearing his throat, Profe says, "You, Benji, and Santiago should go back to the side-by-side and keep an eye on Mr. Gearhart."

"But I want to help!" I say.

"And it's not like Mr. Gearhart is going anywhere," Benji adds.

"But tranquilizer . . . wears off," Santiago says, looking back at the body bag resting in the side-by-side.

Profe waves his hand at the side-by-side. "You're right. We can't leave a cadaver unattended in the middle of campus. Y'all watch it for us while Dr. Tanaka and I take care of Ms. Soto."

Benji pouts as we trudge back to the side-by-side. Santiago looks relieved to not have to go head-to-head with Ms. Soto and part of me agrees with him. We settle into the side-by-side, and I stare at Mr. Gearhart's body bag, examining it for any sign of movement. It lies still . . . for now.

"Go left! Don't let her sweep your legs!" we hear Captain Reynolds shout from the stadium.

Benji looks at me, but Arañita has already taken off thinking of Profe flying through the air after a hit from Ms. Soto, to Captain Reynolds calling the medics to the stadium, to a million other things.

"I'm not like her, am I?" I say out loud. I put my ponytail over my shoulder and inspect it for split ends.

Santiago pokes me in the back with his finger. "More . . . information," he says.

I take a deep breath and turn in my seat toward Benji and Santiago. "Pilar. I'm not like her, am I?"

Benji raises an eyebrow. "Why would you possibly think that? She's a dumpling with no filling. Or maybe a game controller without batteries."

"An empty . . . enchilada," Santiago adds. "A skateboard . . . with no wheels."

I shake my head. "But she's always saying how my brain is just like hers. I swear every day she tells me how much we're alike."

"We need helmets!" Dr. Tanaka's voice comes from the stadium, and I hear a loud grunt.

I pick at a hangnail on my index finger, trying to keep Arañita from replaying every conversation I've ever had with Pilar. "Think they're okay out there?"

Santiago grunts. "Don't change . . . the subject."

Benji nods and nudges me with his elbow. "You may both have different ways of thinking, but everyone does, really. A girl in my history class last year had synesthesia. Like she thinks of colors when she hears different words. She told me that whenever she heard my name, she saw light purple. I love that."

He shifts in his seat and faces me. "And there were like three kids in my English class with dyslexia. One of them did the most amazing report on a book where this kid can talk to animals."

Santiago nudges me again. "My brain . . . is full of maggots. We all . . . think different."

I bite my lip. Benji and Santiago don't understand. They don't get that I'm pretty sure Pilar has an Arañita of her own. Except her Arañita told her to do terrible things. Will my Arañita betray me like that?

"Stop her!" Profe shouts.

We look up just in time to see Ms. Soto stumble from the stadium entrance, grunting as she speeds toward us. Profe, Dr. Tanaka, and Captain Reynolds chase after her, out of breath.

Ms. Soto's onesie is torn at the shoulder, revealing her completely exposed collarbone underneath. She's missing three fingers from her left hand and the toes on her right foot are totally gone, giving her a slight limp. But none of that slows her down. She barrels toward us, and we jump from the side-by-side. Santiago steps in front of me but I push him aside.

"She'll completely dislocate every bone in your body," I tell him.

"What do we do?" Benji shouts as Ms. Soto moves closer and closer.

"Frani!" Profe yells.

He slides his tranquilizer gun across the pavement to me and it hits my foot. I pick it up just as Ms. Soto reaches out a muscled right arm, her fingers pointing in unnatural directions, broken from one of her hits. I point the tranquilizer gun directly at her and pull the trigger.

A dart with a pink puff on the end slams just above Ms. Soto's right eye. Her mouth drops open, and a gurgle rises from her throat. She takes three more shuffling steps forward, and I'm afraid she's going to slam into me. Santiago steps between us, and Ms. Soto grabs his hoodie as she falls to the ground, ripping his arm from its socket.

"Oh my god, what are you doing?" a voice screams behind me.

I turn and see Essie, her eyes wide as she takes in the decomposed woman I shot with a dart and Santiago standing above her, his arm lying at his feet.

TWENTY

THE SCREAM ERUPTING from Essie's throat almost bursts my eardrums. Benji crouches down, hands to his head, and squeezes his eyes shut. Santiago is too busy collecting his arm from the ground to pay attention to my sister.

Profe rushes over to her and places his hands on her shoulders. "It's okay, Essie. I can explain everything."

Essie's chest heaves, her eyes still darting from Santiago to Ms. Soto sprawled on the ground.

"What are you doing? What is going on?" Essie asks over and over. The notebooks in her hands are now scattered on the ground.

Dr. Tanaka and Captain Reynolds rush to load Ms. Soto into a body bag. I hop up to help when Captain Reynolds takes a step back to keep from throwing up.

Profe sits Essie down on a bench and proceeds to tell her everything about the reanimated cadavers and our mission to round up all the DUDs. Benji collects Essie's stray notebooks and hands them to her. She takes them without looking at him. When Dr. Tanaka and I lift Ms. Soto's body bag into the side-by-side, Profe explains Pilar's experiments and says to Essie, "Pilar realized if she inserted genetically modified beetles into the cadavers, she could restart their brains."

"Can you imagine brushing against an electric eel while you're swimming? I'm double-checking the ocean from now on," I blurt out.

Essie closes her eyes and rubs her temples. "So, what exactly are you doing now?"

I jut my finger at the body bags on the side-by-side. "We're three down, two to go—"

"No, I don't need to hear it from you," Essie interrupts. "You're not going to make any sense."

I swallow hard.

"Essie, enough," Profe says, his tone firmer than normal.

She snaps her mouth shut.

"Is she up to speed?" Captain Reynolds approaches Profe and Essie.

Profe nods, but Essie can't stop staring at Santiago as he cradles his arm, the color draining from her face.

"Well, we've still got two out there somewhere," Dr. Tanaka says. "Mr. Hutchinson and Ms. Prado."

I look up at the dark blue sky. The lights along the walkway have turned on, casting our shadows across the concrete. "How difficult do you think it will be to find two DUDs in the dark?"

Benji slides his phone into his back pocket and says to his dad, "Unless you can convince Mom otherwise, count me out. She told me I have to come home. Apparently, the moving boxes in my room didn't magically unpack themselves."

Santiago chuckles from his seat in the side-by-side. "You got . . . busted."

Essie's eyes grow wide as she takes in the decomposing gash on Santiago's cheek, his missing finger, and his arm sitting lifeless in his lap.

"Captain Reynolds!" a voice shouts from the stadium.

We turn and see a man in a red polo and tight gray shorts march toward us.

"Did you really put that woman in a body bag?" the man shouts, the silver whistle around his neck flinging side to side as he stomps toward us. "What in tarnation is going on here?"

"Coach Colson, I can explain," Captain Reynolds says.

But before he can, Profe's phone rings.

I stand next to him as he answers and puts it on speaker.

"Professor Gonzalez, this is Melina Stone from the *San Zavala Register*. We're doing a story on some incidents on campus. It appears that strange-looking individuals have been disrupting things at the university. Their appearance suggests they may be from the forensic anthropology facility. Would you care to comment?"

Profe clears his throat and straightens his shoulders. After a moment, he says, "I don't think I have anything to say at this time. No comment."

He hangs up the phone and slides it into the pocket of his shirt.

Benji leans over to Profe.

"Sir, it seems like too many people are finding out too many things too quickly," he says.

What's your current status, Frani?

I check my phone as I chew on a dry strawberry Pop-Tart. I start to type an answer, but Arañita flies across her web. I type and delete my response three times, realizing that I've double-typed words, left other words completely out, and forgotten entire sentences I wanted to tell Benji.

Arañita doesn't make it easy to type when I have a lot to say.

Status? Santiago and his arm slept in the freezer with Mr. Gearhart, Mr. Zimmerman, and Ms. Soto. Captain Reynolds is still coming up with a story to tell Coach Colson about the body bags. And the newspaper won't stop contacting Profe for a comment about the strange things on campus.

The coffee maker beeps and pulls me from my phone. Profe shuffles out of his room, his eyes barely open. I hop up and pour a large mug of coffee for him.

My phone buzzes again.

Wish I could help but Mom says I have to spend the day cleaning my room and doing my laundry because apparently it's rude to wear the same T-shirt three days in a row.

I chuckle, imagining Benji's grungy *Death Note* T-shirt as I hand Profe his coffee.

We're trying to find Mr. Hutchinson today, I type back. He was some kind of fisherman on the Gulf Coast when he was alive. Think he might be near the riverbank like Mr. Gearhart was?

Profe sits down next to me at the kitchen table and rubs his temples. I'm not sure he slept at all last night. When he wasn't dodging emails and calls from TV stations, newspapers, and university officials, he was trying to figure out where to find our two remaining DUDs. And what to do with the DUDs we'd already rounded up, especially since they'd started to wiggle around in their body bags before we put them in the freezer with Santiago.

I'll FaceTime you when I'm done with the list of chores Mom wants me to do. I'm pretty sure it's longer than my kill streak in Brain Bashers 3, Benji responds.

I turn my phone over on the table and stare at Profe. The dark circles under his eyes make him look slightly like a DUD.

"Plan today?" I ask him, passing him my other Pop-Tart.

He takes a bite and coughs, sending crumbs across the table. Sighing, he brushes the crumbs away with his hand. "Got a call from Captain Reynolds this morning. The folks at the San Zavala Aquatic Research Center called him—"

"I love axolotls!" I interrupt.

Profe sets his Pop-Tart down.

"Sorry," I say.

The aquatic center in town has entire tanks of axolotls that look like pink and brown salamanders wearing frilly wigs.

Profe clears his throat and Arañita quits replaying my second-grade field trip to the aquatic center. "Captain Reynolds said the aquatic center had a strange visitor early this morning who waded into one of the research pools. Based on the description, there's a possibility it might be Mr. Hutchinson. So, he and I are going there to round up our fourth cadaver."

"I can help!" I say, quickly throwing away my Pop-Tart wrapper and brushing crumbs off my shorts.

Profe shakes his head. "No, I need you to stay here and help Dr. Tanaka. He's working on possible solutions for our reanimated cadavers. He might need your assistance."

I purse my lips. This is the second time that Profe has turned me down. I can't help but hear Essie's voice in my head that I'm not doing a good job, that I'm too distracted. Maybe Profe is afraid I'll make too many mistakes. And he won't understand it's all Arañita's fault.

"Does that work for you, Frani?" Profe asks.

I nod slowly. "Yeah, I guess."

It's hard to hide my disappointment.

After Profe leaves, I head out to the lab. When I get there, Dr. Tanaka is examining Santiago, who is sitting on a stool, his shirt off and over his lap. The skin on his chest is yellowish gray and saggy, as if Santiago shrank three sizes. Dr. Tanaka pulls a long thread and snips it with a pair of scissors.

"There you go," he says to Santiago. "Good as new."

Santiago looks down at his arm, which Dr. Tanaka sewed back on. He rolls his shoulder slowly, but his arm doesn't move. Staring at his hand, he tries to wiggle his fingers. Nothing happens.

"New?" he asks Dr. Tanaka. "I don't think . . . I'll be entering a basketball tournament . . . any time soon."

Dr. Tanaka clears his throat. "Um, it's only cosmetic. It won't be able to move like a regular arm since the muscles and blood vessels are dead. It's just so we don't have a spare arm lying around."

"Will this . . . keep happening?" Santiago asks, his mouth sagging as his eyebrows press together.

I walk over to them. "Will what keep happening?"

Santiago lifts his left arm with his right hand and lets it

drop lifeless to his lap. "Body parts . . . dropping. The world's worst . . . birthday piñata."

I shake my head. "We're gonna figure something out. Don't worry."

Grimacing, Santiago takes a deep breath. "You keep . . . saying that. But what's . . . the plan?"

I chew on the inside of my mouth, thinking. Glancing at Dr. Tanaka, I shrug my shoulders. Instead of dazzling us with his own ideas, Dr. Tanaka walks over to the freezer door and opens it. Rolling out a long cart with a body bag on it, he says, "We've got something else to figure out too."

When he stops the cart in front of us, I notice that the end of the body bag is slightly moving, the cadaver inside wiggling their feet.

"The freezer didn't do much," Dr. Tanaka says. "The tranquilizer wore off and they're waking up. We need to find a permanent solution that doesn't damage their bodies."

"Smart," I say. "Since Benji's first instinct would probably be to bash their brains in with an oversized encyclopedia."

Santiago looks at me with wide eyes.

"Sorry," I tell him.

I grab a laptop from Profe's desk and sit next to Santiago. Dr. Tanaka settles into his desk in the lab and opens a notebook, scribbling away. I've never understood how he can brainstorm by handwriting things, but I guess everyone works differently.

"What should . . . we look for?" Santiago asks.

I hover my hand over the laptop keyboard, unsure of what to type.

Dr. Tanaka turns to us in his chair. "The way I'm thinking about it, we need something that will stop the electrical activity happening in the cadavers' brains. That's what reanimated them in the first place with Pilar's electric eel–scarab beetle creation."

I nod as Dr. Tanaka goes back to work. I type on the keyboard and Story Stack pops up.

"This . . . will help?" Santiago says to me.

"It doesn't hurt to check and see if anyone commented on my post. Maybe someone knows you," I whisper to him as I scroll through the website.

I click on my post about Santiago and show him a comment someone made about how Santiago helped them in math class. They said they went to high school with him and tutored him after school. He gave them Takis when they got an answer correct.

"Do you remember doing that?" I ask him.

Santiago closes his eyes and takes a deep breath, thinking. I sit and watch him, biting my lip so I don't blurt out anything and ruin his concentration. The air conditioner clicks on in the lab and cold air washes over us.

Santiago finally opens his eyes and shakes his head. "No," he says. "I wish . . . I did. This would be easier . . . if my brain wasn't useless . . . right?"

I take a deep breath. "I know what that feels like."

Before I can look at any of the other comments on my post, Dr. Tanaka rushes over to us. "Just got a call from Profe. He and Captain Reynolds need help rounding up Mr. Hutchinson at the aquatic center. Think you can handle things here? If the cadavers start to move too much again, just inject them in the temple with more tranquilizer. Sound good?"

I drum my fingers on the table. "Does Profe need my help too?"

Dr. Tanaka shakes his head. "No, he said for you to stay here."

My shoulders sink. Nobody wants my help. And Arañita is probably the reason why. "Okay. Well, be careful."

Dr. Tanaka rushes out and Santiago and I get back to work. We scroll through website after website on my laptop but nothing helpful pops up. A notification appears in the corner of the screen, alerting me that the laptop is almost out of battery. I hop up to get the charging cord.

The air conditioner whirs in the background along with the clicking of the centrifuge separating samples from cadavers and the row of computers scanning data Profe loaded into them. I plug my laptop into the outlet behind us.

A loud snap fills the lab and we're plunged into darkness.

"What . . . happened?" Santiago asks.

I feel my way over to the main lab door, where a rectangular panel is set into the wall, only bumping my hip on the tables and desks three times.

"We had too many things running. It kicked one of the breakers," I say, opening the door of the panel and flipping a switch. Light floods the lab again.

"Oops," Santiago says.

Arañita plucks at a string so hard, I almost double over.

"Nope. Not oops. I just figured out how to keep these cadavers from ever reanimating again."

TWENTY-ONE

SANTIAGO AND I stand in front of the side-by-side as I hold a pair of jumper cables.

"Explain again. . . . Maybe less words . . . this time," Santiago says, staring at me as I point to the battery on the side-by-side. The word flood I drowned Santiago with when I first came up with my idea probably made as much sense as a hammer made of marshmallows.

"Maggot nostrils. Sorry," I tell him. "Okay, so just like how we overloaded the circuit breaker in the lab with too much electricity, we can overload the DUDs and cause them to lose power. The currents in their brains will switch off because of the sudden surge in electricity."

Santiago purses his lips. They're completely cracked, and his bottom lip is starting to sag away from his gums. "How do we . . . do that? I don't think we have . . . enough electric eels . . . Or any."

I hold up the jumper cables. "Did you ever have to restart

a dead battery in a car? One time, Profe left the lights on in the truck when we were out in the field, and it drained the battery. Dr. Tanaka had to come out in the side-by-side and use these cables to restart the truck."

"Why do we want . . . to restart the DUDs?" Santiago asks. "That already . . . happened. It wasn't good the first time . . . it'll be even worse the second."

I try not to get frustrated at Santiago's questions, but each time he makes me stop explaining, Arañita loses track of where she was skipping on her thread.

I take a deep breath. "It won't restart them. Cars and trucks can handle a sudden burst of electricity. People can't. If we hook up these jumper cables to the side-by-side's battery and then touch the cables to the DUDs, the electrical charge will short-circuit them. They won't feel any pain and we won't have any more reanimated brains."

Santiago nods slowly but takes a step back from the jumper cables in my hand. "Sounds like . . . a plan. A supercharged plan."

"What plan?" a voice says behind us.

I turn and see Essie, her arms crossed and a scowl on her face. "What are you talking about?" she says, making a point of not looking at Santiago.

"I figured out how to stop the DUDs from reanimating. And I'm pretty sure I know where the last one is. Santiago and I are going to round her up."

Essie places her hands on her hips and narrows her eyes at me.

"I'm going with you."

Essie insists on driving onto campus because she says I'll probably get distracted by the cows in the agricultural center and crash the side-by-side. She makes me repeat my plan to her three times, which is frustrating because I leave out information and add totally unrelated things each time.

And she makes Santiago sit in the back seat, so she doesn't have to look at him.

"Tell me why you think this body is at the art building," Essie says, gripping the steering wheel of the side-by-side so hard, I think her knuckles might burst through her skin.

But that's already happened to Santiago.

While we're driving, Profe texts me that they rounded up Mr. Hutchinson and are taking him back to the lab. I don't tell him what we're doing. I want to show him I can bring a DUD back too. I take a deep breath and tap the file from the lab on my lap. "Ms. Prado's information said she was an artist. We realized that the DUDs are drawn to things from when they were alive. I thought Ms. Prado would want to be around art."

"It's a . . . good plan," Santiago says behind me.

Essie grunts. "If you could not talk, that would be great, thanks. I'm just trying to keep my sister from getting demolished by some lab experiment."

I clench my fists. "Don't talk to Santiago like that."

Santiago takes a deep breath. I glance at him, and he smirks. "I probably shouldn't mention . . . your left arm looks like . . . a tasty pork roast," he says to Essie.

Raising her eyebrow, Essie slams on the brakes of the side-by-side. I launch forward and brace my hand against the glove box. My wrist stings.

"Overreact much? He's just kidding. I think," I say, shaking out my hand.

Essie rolls her eyes. "We're here."

I look at the two-story stone building in front of us. A large glass window reveals paintings and sculptures inside.

Santiago slowly gets out of the side-by-side, giving Essie lots of space.

"Okay, so we have to figure out a way to draw Ms. Prado here so we can shock her with the jumper cables," I explain.

Essie sighs. "You already said that three times."

"Then we do it . . . three times," Santiago says.

I smile at him while Essie scowls.

"Okay, I'll go around the left side of the building," I say. "Essie, you and Santiago can go around the right side. Check and see if Ms. Prado is anywhere."

Essie shakes her head. "I'm not teaming up with him. Besides, I need to stay by you to make sure you don't get distracted by a bird, a grasshopper, or whatever."

I swallow hard, wishing I could come up with something to say back to Essie, but Arañita started thinking about birds and grasshoppers the second Essie mentioned them. And I hate her for it.

Santiago waves a four-fingered hand at me before disappearing around the right side of the art building. I go around the left side and Essie follows me.

"How are you even going to get this thing to follow you back to the side-by-side if you do find it?" she says. "You think it's just going to stand there and wait for you to electrocute it?"

I clench my fists at my sides and concentrate on the ground, trying to keep Arañita from taking off in all directions to come up with sixteen separate answers to Essie's questions. But it wouldn't matter. She never has confidence in any of my ideas.

We don't see anyone near the art building, but it's Sunday, so I wouldn't expect a lot of students or professors around. There are a few flyers taped to the windows for a Students for a Broccoli-Free Society picnic happening in a couple of days, and my heart beats faster thinking about the flood of students on campus with all the DUDs.

I peek in one of the windows and see three large paintings hanging on a white wall in front of a twisty metal sculpture. But no one seems to be inside the building either.

"Well, this is going about as well as I expected," Essie huffs.

When we reach the back of the building, Santiago is standing there. He shrugs, but only his right arm moves. "I don't . . . see her," he says, and then chuckles. "The DUD is MIA . . . at CTU."

Essie blows her hair off her forehead with a frustrated sigh. "Now what? What's your big plan? Think you can come up with something that won't be a complete disaster?"

"Shut up!" I shout. "I can't think with your constant questions!"

"You can't ever think!" Essie shoots back.

That's when we hear the growl.

It comes from above us. I look up and see someone standing on the balcony of the art building's second floor.

"Is that . . . her?" Santiago asks, wincing as he twists his neck to raise his gaze to the balcony.

"Pretty sure the number of women in bright pink bathrobes wandering around campus is usually zero. So that's definitely Ms. Prado," I say.

In Ms. Prado's files, Dr. Tanaka wrote that he dressed Ms. Prado in a robe because he wanted to study the effects of linen on decomposing skin.

"Well, how do we get it down from there?" Essie asks.

As if answering Essie's question, Ms. Prado grunts and throws herself against the balcony railing. Her momentum thrusts her over the side and her body sails through the air toward us.

And lands right on top of Essie.

Essie screams, and I run over to her, pulling her by the arms out from under Ms. Prado. The force of impact on Ms. Prado's body was less than gentle, her left leg now slightly twisted and her collarbone poking through the skin. Essie seems to have broken Ms. Prado's fall and kept her from damaging herself more.

Essie pushes me away and screams again. Santiago moves toward Ms. Prado, and she stops shuffling toward him with her twisted leg, her hands absentmindedly brushing along the pink fabric of her robe. Ms. Prado takes two quick steps forward, holding the robe out behind her.

"Does she think . . . it's a cape?" Santiago asks. "Is she a . . . super DUD?"

I chuckle and Essie punches me hard in the arm. "Not funny. It almost flattened me on the sidewalk."

Ms. Prado bounces on her heels, her ankles popping with the movement.

"We have to get her close to the side-by-side," I say. "That's the only way the jumper cables will reach her."

Ms. Prado flings the robe behind her again and makes a small hop off the ground. When she lands, her left shinbone cracks and she stumbles to the side. I picture her twirling and dancing as she created her paintings, music filling her studio. I imagine her creating large portraits of the people she loved, capturing their smiles with her brushes.

“Frani! What are you doing?” Essie’s shout snaps me from my thoughts.

Ms. Prado stumbles after Essie.

“Lead her . . . to the front,” Santiago calls, his voice scratchy and barely a shout. “You’re our . . . tasty bait.”

“Don’t tell me what to do!” Essie screeches as she runs around the side of the building.

I chase after her, passing Ms. Prado, who’s still flinging the bathrobe behind her and making small jumps off the ground. Each time she lands, I hear another crack in her legs.

When we finally reach the side-by-side, I pull the jumper cables out and open the front hood, revealing the battery. Essie pushes me and grabs the cables.

“You’re just going to mess it up,” she scowls. “And I don’t know CPR well enough if you electrocute yourself.”

“No, I’m not going to mess up,” I say, yanking the cables back.

“You can’t do anything right! Not with how much you space out! You’re going to get hurt.”

We’re so busy arguing, we don’t notice Ms. Prado is right behind us now. She growls, revealing only three jagged yellow teeth and split lips. Reaching out a hand to us, she slashes at Essie.

Before Ms. Prado can make contact, Santiago comes up

behind her. With his one good arm, he reaches around her waist and pushes her away from us. The motion twists his body and he grunts as his ankle wrenches to the side. He falls to the ground and Ms. Prado lands on top of him.

I'm so busy staring at the bone sticking out from Santiago's ankle, I don't feel Essie yank the cables from my hand. She connects them to the side-by-side's battery and lunges toward Ms. Prado.

"Wait!" I shout, realizing that Santiago will get shocked too since Ms. Prado is still on top of him.

I roll Ms. Prado's body away from Santiago but trip on her robe and fall to the ground. The concrete scratches my elbows and knees. Essie touches the metal claws of the jumper cables to Ms. Prado's exposed stomach. Her body jerks as her arms and legs contract. Her spine rolls up and then she lies still.

Essie detaches the jumper cables from the battery as I pick a small rock from the bleeding scratch on my knee. After she tosses the cables back into the side-by-side, she flips open Ms. Prado's file, which is lying on my seat.

"Oh, you've got to be kidding me. It says right here that Emiliana Prado was a skydiver, performing at air shows across the country. She took up painting after she retired. You got it all wrong because you couldn't concentrate long enough to read all the information," Essie says, throwing the file at me. The papers scatter all over the pavement. "She could've really hurt you. Don't you get it? I know you and Dad have your own little club with all this dead stuff, but you have to actually pay attention and be careful."

I pick up a paper next to me and see that it says Ms. Prado was one of the top skydivers, jumping out of all kinds of airplanes. And sometimes art buildings too, it seems. She wasn't dancing in the bathrobe. She was trying to use it as a parachute and jump.

Crumpling the paper in my hands, I squeeze my eyes shut, trying to remember if I read the entire file about Ms. Prado. I'm sure I did. But I can't picture myself doing it. Arañita just jumped straight to one paragraph and forgot the rest even existed.

"You were too distracted to see the DUD up on that ledge, to read all the information, or to complete your stupid plan the way it was supposed to be," Essie says, crossing her arms and stomping her foot on the ground. "Can you do anything right without putting yourself and everyone else in danger?"

I open my eyes and see Santiago sprawled on the ground, his left foot twisted at an unnatural angle. Ms. Prado lies next to him, a small pool of black liquid seeping out of her ear.

My knees and elbows sting from falling on the concrete

and I'm out of breath. Arañita slams around inside my brain, overwhelmed by everything that happened.

"Well?" Essie says. "What do you have to say for yourself?"

I look up at her and slowly stand.

"Nothing," I say.

And then I run away.

TWENTY-TWO

I RACE THROUGH campus, my feet stinging in my shoes as they slap against the concrete. I'm out of breath, but I don't stop. The library is a blur as I run past. My ears ring with Essie's words.

Can you do anything right?

Arañita bounces around my brain so quickly, I can't rest on a single thought.

So I keep running as she replays my greatest hits.

That time in second grade when I got lost on a field trip to the San Zavala Zoo because I was distracted by the fluffy hair on the tamarins and didn't notice my group walking away. My teacher called Profe and went on and on about how I was irresponsible.

In third grade, Profe got a call from the principal because I was late to school more often than I was on time. Getting ready in the morning is always a challenge. I head to the bathroom to brush my teeth but end up taking the water cup from my room to the kitchen. In the kitchen I see that the magnets on the fridge can be rearranged to spell a word to call Essie. Once I do that, I spot my Converse by the front door and decide to relace them in a different pattern. By the time I realize I haven't brushed my teeth yet, I've already missed the bus.

I took up crochet last year but had so many incomplete projects, Profe refused to buy me any more yarn. Same with learning how to play the flute, trying out for basketball, and enrolling in watercolor classes. I was always excited when I started. It was the only thing I could think about. But then that feeling just . . . went away. And Essie got frustrated with the sheet music, basketballs, and paints left all over the house.

My lungs burn, and I skid to a stop, putting my hands on my knees as my chest heaves. Tears pool in my eyes and stream down my cheeks when I blink. I look up and see the CTU Police Department building, the live oak trees covering most of the stone.

Brushing my hair off my sweaty face, I push through the front doors.

Sergeant Cho looks me up and down as I walk over to her desk.

"You okay there, Frani?" she asks, tapping her pen on a clipboard.

I nod and take a deep breath.

"Can I talk to Pilar Estrada? Is she still here?" I pick at

the edge of my T-shirt and try to look at the sergeant instead of at every flyer hanging in the entryway.

Sergeant Cho purses her lips. "We're waiting for the Cerro County Police Department to pick her up. She's still in a holding cell. Captain Reynolds sure took a long time figuring out what to charge her with, but you didn't hear that from me."

Raising an eyebrow, she leans over the desk between us and whispers, "Is it true what she did? That all the problems on campus are because she made zombies?"

I drum my fingers on the counter between us. "I'm not sure. That's what I wanted to talk to her about."

"Your dad knows you're here?" Sergeant Cho asks.

I nod. "Of course. He's busy with things at the lab so he sent me to ask her some questions and get information we need."

Sergeant Cho searches my face as she pulls a key ring off her belt. "Yeah, I gotta run errands for the higher-ups all the time too. Follow me. Just don't stay long; they shouldn't have sent a kid to talk to a possible criminal. But that's just my opinion."

She leads me through a door and down a bare hallway. Punching a code into a keypad, she opens another door and motions me through. On the right is a long row of small cells, each with a bench lining the far wall.

"Is Pilar the only one in here right now?" I ask, my

stomach starting to flip-flop.

Sergeant Cho shakes her head. "There's a kid in the cell at the end of the hall who decided to free all the lab rats from the biology building and let them loose in the dean's office. I think he was upset about a test grade or something."

"That seems like a bit of an overreaction," I say.

Sergeant Cho gets a chair and sets it in front of the second cell. "Here you go," she says. "If you need anything, just hit that buzzer by the door."

I settle into the chair, relieved for a break after running around campus. Peering into the cell, I see Pilar sitting on the bench on the other side. She looks up at me and scrunches her eyebrows together.

"What are you doing here?" she asks, her voice scratchy.

I wrap my feet around the legs of the chair and pick at a loose thread on my shorts. "I need to talk to you."

Pilar crosses her arms and scowls. "I'm not saying anything, Frani Fran."

"Don't call me that," I mumble, staring at my lap instead of Pilar.

We sit in silence, and I count the bricks in the wall behind Pilar and the bars in the cell. I listen to the Rat Thief snoring three cells down. I let Arañita bounce along her web, even though my brain is tired and I just want to rest. I scratch at a mosquito bite on my wrist, and it gets redder and redder.

"The snake venom probably helped," I mutter. "That's probably why Santiago is so strong."

"What?"

I glance at Pilar. "I wasn't talking to you. I was talking to myself."

"Snake venom. Got it," Pilar says. "Are they still out there, wandering around?"

Her voice almost sounds excited as her eyes sparkle.

I roll my eyes. "Yes, we're almost done cleaning up your mess."

Pilar sighs. "Perfectly good specimens ruined. All my research down the drain. It's a shame, really. All because none of you understands what I was doing."

"You know, the villain's monologue in *Crocodile Cyborgs 4* was way too long. The movie could've been ten minutes shorter," I blurt out, and then immediately clench my fists, mad at Arañita for saying something so stupid.

Chuckling, Pilar uncrosses her arms. "That's a jump. I won't ask you how you got from Point A to Point H. It's too annoying to have to retrace our steps, isn't it?"

I bite my lip to keep myself from saying the twenty-three thoughts Arañita is trying to push out of my mouth. And I don't want to agree with Pilar.

She takes a deep breath and taps her foot on the floor. "You know, the whole time I was in school, my teachers told me constantly that I'd never be able to focus on anything long enough to get good at it. They said I'd be lucky if I graduated high school and that there was no way I was going to college. But look at me now. People just don't understand us, do they? They don't understand how we think."

I stay quiet. In my mind, Arañita shows my teachers getting mad at me for drawing in the margins of my paper, even though it helps me focus. She gives me a slideshow of classmates who aren't friends with me anymore because they think I blurt out weird things or I'm not interested in what we first bonded over anymore. Arañita plucks at a thin thread that tells me Pilar is right.

I finally look at her sitting on the bench. She flips her black hair over her shoulder.

"Did I ever tell you about the time I stayed up all night to work on a project for my entomology class when I was a freshman?" Pilar says. "Didn't even need coffee. I loved reading about bugs so much that I didn't notice I'd been awake for eight hours putting all my information together."

"I've done stuff like that before," I say, immediately hating myself for having a friendly conversation with the person who caused so much trouble at the body farm.

"What was it for you?" Pilar asks. "What got you so excited that you couldn't stop thinking about it?"

I roll my shoulders. "Writing stories. It's the only time I feel like Arañita calms down. It's the one thing I haven't gotten tired of and kept doing for the longest amount of time."

"Arañita?" Pilar asks, raising an eyebrow.

I bite my nails, trying to think of an explanation when Arañita is twisting the threads of her web together in a tight knot.

"She's . . . she's why my brain works the way it does," I mumble, unsure if Pilar will understand my explanation.

Instead, she claps and startles me. "That's wonderful!"

Pilar taps her fingers against her lips, thinking. "I wish I had an Arañita when I was your age. All I had were teachers telling my parents I needed to see a counselor and a mom and dad who wanted me to take pills to control me."

I swallow hard. Several of my teachers have told Profe I should meet with a therapist. I even met with one a few times in fifth grade. Profe and I have also had lots of talks about maybe going on medicine to help me feel better.

"Don't do it, Frani," Pilar says, as if reading my mind. She narrows her eyes. "Don't let them erase you. Don't let them take away who you are. What will happen to your Arañita?"

If Arañita was gone, I probably wouldn't be late for school. I'd be able to focus on my homework for more than five minutes at a time. I'd be able to follow along with conversations and wouldn't get distracted planning what I was going to say.

I bite my nail, lost in Arañita's web. "Maybe it would be

okay to get help. I don't know."

"Our brains are amazing. Look at what I've been able to do. Look at what you've done! We can't let anyone take that away from us."

"What I've done?" I mumble.

All I can think is how tired I get because Arañita won't stop bouncing around on her web. How I lost the notebook out in the field and didn't read Ms. Prado's full file. I think about when Profe and Dr. Tanaka didn't want me helping them.

"I couldn't have done my experiment without you, you know," Pilar says. Her eyes narrow, and she smirks at me.

I raise my eyebrow. "What are you talking about?"

"We're the same, Frani. I knew just what buttons of yours to push so you'd distract your dad while I implanted the bug in Mr. Gearhart's brain. Or how to get you off topic so you wouldn't ask me about my missing bugs."

My stomach flips-flops, and I twist my fingers so hard in my lap, my knuckles crack. "You used me."

Pilar waves a dismissive hand. "We're so much better than them, Frani. Trust me. You think your father could come up with my experiment? That Dr. Tanaka would've been able to do what I did? Their boring minds could never accomplish what I did."

Hot bile rises in my throat, and I might throw up. I think

about what Benji said. That everyone's brain is different.

"That's not true," I whisper.

Pilar crosses her arms again. "What?"

Clearing my throat, I sit up in the chair. "That's not true. Profe is one of the smartest people I know. He knows exactly how to look at a problem and figure out the steps to solve it. Dr. Tanaka is kind and understanding. He treats everybody with respect, dead or alive. And, sure, their brains may be different from mine, but that's okay. We all can do amazing things."

Pilar huffs and rolls her eyes. "Whatever. You don't under—"

"No. You don't understand," I interrupt. "I'm not any better or any less than anyone else because of how my brain works. And I'm not going to use Arañita—"

My voice catches in my throat and Pilar looks at me expectantly. I swallow hard and continue. "Never mind. I'm not talking about Arañita. Because she doesn't really exist. I always used her as an excuse for why my brain works the way it does. But it's not her. It's just me. And I'm okay with that."

I think of all the horrible things that Pilar has done, the chaos she's caused, just because she used her brain as an excuse. I think of Santiago and how he got caught up in Pilar's experiment. How even though he's falling apart, the black web of veins on his wrist growing, he still makes jokes and helps me and Benji.

Pilar purses her lips as I stand up. "They're going to try to control you. To erase you."

I shake my head. "I know who I am. I'm Francisca Mirabel Gonzalez. Arañita can completely disappear, and I'll still be me. I can get the help my brain might need by talking to someone or taking medicine, and I'll still be one hundred percent me."

I jam the buzzer next to the door and a loud sound fills the room.

"And I'm nothing like you."

TWENTY-THREE

WHEN I STEP out of the police department building, Benji is waiting for me.

"I figured out how Santiago died," I tell him, knowing we've hung out enough now for him to be used to me not saying hi.

He raises his eyebrow. "Really?"

"Yep. I put two and two together. Or rattlesnakes and wounds together," I say. Then I stop myself. "Wait. How are you here right now?"

Benji puts his hands on his hips and squares his shoulders like a superhero. "I was a chore-completing machine! I wondered where you might be because you weren't answering your phone and then Dad said you'd had him put a 'find my phone' on his phone for you because you kept losing it. The tracker showed you were here."

"Brilliant," I say. "So you wanna hear what I figured out?"

"Of course," Benji says as I hop onto the back of his bike

and he pedals through campus.

"Okay, here's our evidence. Remember when we first saw Santiago, he had a wound on his wrist that looked like a bad spider or snake bite?"

Benji nods, already out of breath from pedaling.

"And then when I went out in the field with your dad, we had to avoid a nest of baby rattlesnakes."

Benji huffs in response as he pedals faster.

"So, putting those two things together, I think that Santiago accidentally got bitten by the rattlesnakes. Like maybe he tripped and fell, and his hand ended up in the nest. It doesn't take long for baby snakes to do a lot of damage. And if he was out there all by himself, no one would be able to help him. The venom would've been too quick. Pilar's lost bug could've found him lying on the rocks and crawled in his ear or something."

We ride on in silence, and I listen to Benji's heavy breathing as he pedals. I know we're both thinking of our new friend and what happened to him. As we continue through campus, my brain is still churning. Not Arañita, just my brain.

"Do you think Santiago is different from the other DUDs because of the snake venom? Like that interacted with Pilar's beetles and made him more human and less DUDish?" I ask.

Benji nods as I grip the sides of his T-shirt for balance. I can see the sweat pooling on his back. "I guess. If there's one thing the last week has shown me, it's that anything is possible. Including snake venom creating superpowered zombies."

I chuckle. "You said the Z-word."

He shrugs.

My phone buzzes in my back pocket and I take it out, almost toppling Benji and me over on his bike.

A text from Essie stares back at me.

Your undead thing ran off looking for you after we got back to the lab with that other body. Might want to round it up before it causes any more problems. You need to be more responsible.

I tap Benji on the shoulder. "Stop," I tell him. "Santiago ran off. We've got to find him."

Benji leans over his handlebars, catching his breath. "Where do you think he might be?"

Hopping off Benji's bike, I look around campus. There are several students wandering around but I don't hear any screams in the distance from anyone who's run into a decomposing body shuffling down the sidewalk.

I have no idea where Santiago could be.

Absentmindedly opening the Story Stack on my phone, I click on my post about Santiago to check if there are any new comments. There are a few that say they hope we find his family and one that says they went to school with him in Oregon. I don't think Santiago's ever been to Oregon. But the last comment sticks out.

> I think I was in a foster home with Santiago in Corpus Christi. He always helped take care of the younger kids in the house. He taught me how to make a quesadilla in the microwave and macaroni and cheese on the stove without burning myself. But any time he wasn't helping out, he was down at one of the docks in town fishing. I think he liked being near the water more than anything else. I hope you figure everything out with him.

I show the comment to Benji, and he bites his lip.

"Santiago liked fishing?" he asks.

"And easy cooking," I say with a smile. Benji and I have that in common with him.

Sliding my phone into my pocket, I look up and down the sidewalk. "Cooking and fishing. If you liked those two things, where on campus would you go?"

"The culinary building?" Benji asks.

I shake my head. "I don't think that's simple cooking. That's like eight-layer wedding cake, fancy steak, and French words we can't even pronounce. Not exactly microwaved tortillas."

Benji stretches his legs. "I don't think I can bike all the way to Corpus Christi. That'll take like a whole week to get to the coast, right?"

My brain races through all the places on campus, getting distracted thinking about the time Profe took me to see *Hadestown* at the performing arts center, when I almost got stuck between the sliding bookcases in the library, and when Captain Reynolds let me watch water rescue practice down at the San Zavala River dock.

"That's it!" I say.

Benji looks at me with raised eyebrows. "Whatever it is, will it take a long time to pedal there?"

I motion him to the back of the bike and settle in on the seat. "My turn. We're heading to the river."

I pedal us past the math building and the student center as Benji grips my shoulders. The warm summer air blows my ponytail in his face.

My leg muscles burn and my lungs might explode like overfilled water balloons, but we finally get to the university park on the banks of the San Zavala River. There are several picnic benches and next to each is a small metal grill.

"Those look like they'd be good for simple cooking," I say, pointing to a grill.

Benji looks through the large live oak trees in the park. "But there's no sign of Santiago," he says.

We get off Benji's bike and I prop it up against a tree. I

walk down to the riverbank and see a deflated inner tube that looks like a rock tore a hole in it. Crouching down, I stick a finger in the flowing water. It's cold even though it's hot outside since the river is fed by underground springs. That's why students flock here in warm weather.

Benji walks up behind me. "Where could he be?"

I twirl my finger in the water, making swirling ripples on the surface. "I have no idea. I hope he's okay."

Before we can say anything else, I hear a splash. I look downriver just in time to see a head of black hair slowly descend below the water.

"Was that—" Benji starts to ask, but I don't hear the rest of the question.

I'm already wading into the water and swimming toward the body that disappeared below the surface. Diving down, I open my eyes in the murky water and see Santiago staring back at me, a look of panic on his face. The water immediately bloated his skin, making it puff out like a plumped-up balloon.

Swimming as fast as I can, I reach Santiago and slide my arms under his armpits. I kick my legs hard and push toward the surface, dragging him with me. My lungs strain and I don't know how much longer I can hold my breath. Santiago is a lot heavier than I thought he'd be, and he doesn't seem to be able to move a muscle to help get us to the surface.

I see stars in my eyes and just before I think I might pass out, an arm slips around my waist and yanks me to the surface of the water and onto the riverbank.

Staring up at Benji as I lie in the grass, I wipe my eyes. I cough and spew water in his face. I look next to me and watch Santiago struggle to sit up, a low growl gurgling from his throat. His hair mat slipped off in the water, and he's now completely bald, his skull visible.

One time, Profe had to assist the county police in identifying a body that was pulled from Bluebonnet Lake. He told me it was completely bloated, its eyes swollen shut and its skin dark gray. When they tried to put the cadaver in the body bag, the skin on the arms slipped completely off.

Profe didn't let me come along on that trip.

"Oh wow," Benji whispers, staring at the ground. "That's . . . a lot to look at."

Santiago's gray hoodie is soaked and pulling down on his body. I reach out and squeeze some of the water from the sleeve. Benji grips a handful of wet fabric from Santiago's back and twists, water dripping down his hand. Santiago seems relieved as we lessen the weight of his soaked hoodie pressing down on him.

He looks at me, water seeping from his eye sockets and the cut on his cheek. When he purses his lips, water drips down his chin and his lips thin out.

"Are you okay?" I ask, still squeezing water out of his hoodie.

Santiago sits up straighter.

"I remember," he says. "I remember . . . everything."

TWENTY-FOUR

I NEVER THOUGHT a decomposing cadaver would ever sit at my dining room table, but this hasn't exactly been a normal summer. Santiago slumps in the wooden chair I usually sit in. Profe and I are on either side of him. Dr. Tanaka and Benji pulled chairs from the living room. Essie stands back and leans against the kitchen counter, slowly sipping her Dr Pepper while she eyes Santiago warily.

I had to call Profe to come get us, thankful I remembered to chuck my phone in the grass before I dove in the river. I was afraid if we made Santiago walk to the body farm, he'd completely disintegrate by the time we got there. And Benji and I were tired from biking all over campus anyway.

"So, you remember how you died?" Profe asks. He holds an ophthalmoscope up to Santiago's eye to check him. Santiago's pupil doesn't dilate at all when the bright light from the scope shines on it and the part of his eye that should be white is completely red.

Santiago slowly lifts the sleeve of his hoodie and shows us a black splotch that has grown on his wrist since I first saw it three days ago. "It was this," he says. "Snakes."

"I knew it!" I blurt out, and then give Santiago a sympathetic look. "But how did you even get on the body farm property?"

Santiago thinks for a moment, his eyes slightly closing as if he's trying to remember something in a portion of his brain that's already decomposed. "I ran off. My foster parents . . . we always argued. I was . . . angry."

Dr. Tanaka folds his hands on the table as Benji rests his head on his dad's shoulder. "I'm sorry that happened to you," Dr. Tanaka says.

Slowly nodding, Santiago continues. "I grew up . . . near Corpus Christi. With my grandfather. We used to . . . go fishing all the time."

"That sounds amazing. I keep trying to talk Profe into taking a vacation down to the Gulf, but he's always working," I say, and give Profe a wink.

"Whatever," Essie says behind me. "You'd rather work with bodies than go fishing any day."

I shrug. She's not wrong.

Santiago chuckles, the sound gurgling in his throat. "I fought . . . with my foster parents. I left . . . and just kept walking. I wanted to see . . . the cows on the farm. I always saw them . . . coming from school."

"They are pretty cool," Benji says. "The shaggy ones are my favorite."

"Have you ever seen them stick their tongues up their noses?" I ask. "That's the best. And really hard to do yourself. Trust me."

I wrap my hand around Santiago's hand. His skin feels like tissue paper and I'm afraid I'll grip too hard and tear it.

"I climbed the fence . . . around your farm. I wanted to see . . . what was there. I didn't expect . . . to get bit," Santiago sighs. "I figured I'd die . . . when I was super old . . . out on a fishing boat . . . in the middle of a hurricane."

Glancing out the kitchen window, I stare at the cadavers down the hill under cages and partially buried in the dirt. I wonder how many of them were surprised at dying too.

"Don't worry," I say. "We'll figure out how to fix you. We can make everything better."

Santiago looks down at his hand I'm holding, his pinky finger missing. His left arm hangs lifeless at his side and the cut on his cheek has grown two inches. The light above the table reflects off his exposed skull. He scuffs his shoes on the carpet, and I know that his feet are missing several toes.

"I don't think . . . I'm coming back from this," he says. "This organ piñata . . . has had its last party."

I bite my lip hard, but Santiago squeezes my hand. I can feel the bones in his ring finger pop.

Profe clears his throat. "I think I've figured out how to keep the cadavers we rounded up from reanimating again."

"It took some trial and error, and research into things that I never would've associated with forensic anthropology," Dr. Tanaka says.

"We're not gonna put firecrackers in their brains, are we?" Benji asks. Essie groans and sets her soda can on the counter with more force than usual.

"Or send them to Antarctica to stay permanently frozen?" I add.

Santiago takes a deep breath and nudges me with his elbow. "Always wanted . . . to go there. Maybe . . . play with some penguins."

Dr. Tanaka chuckles and shakes his head. "It's not exactly that. We're using the tranquilizer guns again."

Benji leans toward his dad. "Not to spoil this for you, but we already tried that. It wasn't a permanent solution."

Profe shakes his head. "We're using something different in the injections. We're giving them Botox instead."

Essie laughs and nearly spits her soda out. "The wrinkle medicine? I mean, I think these dead things have terrible complexions, but their appearance seems the least of our problems."

I raise my eyebrow. "Don't they use Botox to help people who have migraines? I mean, I can see these DUDs having a slight headache going from dead to undead."

"My head does . . . hurt a little," Santiago says. "Okay . . . a lot."

"I heard Botox can make you pee less," Benji says. "Like you could play video games for eight hours straight without a bathroom break."

"Are y'all finished? Can I explain?" Profe puts his head in his hands. "As I was saying before so many phenomenal ideas were vomited out here, we can use Botox to permanently cease the cadaver's brain function without causing them any pain or damage to their bodies. It's a little more effective than electricity from the jumper cables you tried on Ms. Soto."

"Because it's a neurotoxin," Dr. Tanaka adds quickly before any of us can offer more uses for the injections.

"What's that?" Santiago whispers to me.

"Well, *neuro* means it has to do with your nervous system, like your brain, and *toxin* is a poison," I explain. "So, a poison for the brain?"

Profe gives me a thumbs-up. "If we inject them with a large enough dose of Botox in the temple, it should stop all their brain function."

Santiago is still holding my hand. His fingers twitch and he shifts slightly in his seat. He looks across the table at Profe.

"Will it . . . hurt?"

Profe shakes his head. "We're not actually using the

tranquilizer guns. It'll be like a shot you get at the doctor. And then just falling asleep. We already tested the theory on Cadaver 072201, Mr. Hutchinson. You wouldn't believe the strange look I got from the medical school when I asked them if I could borrow an EEG machine. We're not supposed to be measuring any brain activity around here."

Dr. Tanaka nods. "After the injection, we attached electrodes to Mr. Hutchinson's temples and watched as the EEG machine slowly showed his brain waves stop. We placed him back out in the field."

Profe keeps looking at Santiago. "It was painless."

I rub the back of Santiago's hand, his skin pulling under my thumb. A lump forms in my throat and I swallow hard. "I wish we could do something," I whisper to him, my voice catching.

Santiago shrugs but his left shoulder doesn't move at all. "We went on . . . an adventure, didn't we?"

Benji smiles. "This was better than my favorite manga. It even had more exposed organs and limbs falling off."

"Best summer . . . ever?" Santiago asks me.

I look at him, but tears start to form in my eyes. I try to think of just the right thing to say, but I can't find it among the fifteen thoughts in my head.

"It's okay," Santiago says, looking at everyone around the table. "I found something . . . I haven't had . . . since my grandfather. Even here . . . at the end."

"What's that?" I ask.

Santiago looks at me and smiles, the left side of his mouth frozen in place.

"A family."

TWENTY-FIVE

SANTIAGO SPENT THE night in the living room again. We turned the thermostat down as much as we could. The house was so cold, I slept in the one sweater I own and three pairs of socks. Essie made a big show about locking her door. Santiago tried to roll his eyes, but they got stuck.

When Santiago, Benji, and I arrive at the lab the next morning, Essie is already there, probably to complain to Profe about having to sleep under the same roof as a DUD. But before she can speak, Profe's booming voice fills the lab.

"She did what?!?"

"Ugh. What now?" Benji asks next to me.

After a few moments, Profe hangs up the phone and turns to us. "I'd say good morning, but that's not true. Pilar escaped from the campus police department before the county police could pick her up. Told Sergeant Cho some story about a stomachache and took an abnormally long time in the bathroom. There was also a break-in at the biology building. Captain Reynolds believes those two things are connected. I agree with him."

Dr. Tanaka groans next to Profe. "How did this happen?"

I think and scuff my shoe on the tile floor of the lab. "This might be my fault."

"What do you mean?" Profe asks.

Taking a deep breath, I explain. "I went to visit Pilar when she was at the CTU Police Department. I mentioned my idea of snake venom making Santiago a stronger DUD. I just blurted it out. It wouldn't surprise me if she's trying to test that hypothesis."

"She just can't help causing problems, can she?" Benji blurts out, rolling his eyes.

I start to say it's not her fault. That the Arañita in her brain is making her chase after ideas that should definitely be ignored. But that's not true. Pilar doesn't have an Arañita. And she's responsible for every idea her brain comes up with, just like everybody else.

Everyone starts talking at the same time about what we should do. It's a lot of noise. All I can manage to do is stare at one of the cadavers in a black body bag on a table in the far corner of the room. Its left foot is moving.

"What was the order?" I ask, still looking at the body bag.

Essie groans. "What on earth are you talking about?"

"What was the order of cadavers that Pilar infected? Do we know that?" I ask, ignoring her.

Dr. Tanaka heads over to one of the computers and clicks

on the screen. "I figured that out. I went through all the surveillance footage we had for each of the cadavers that were reanimated when I suspected Pilar had deleted video of herself infecting the cadavers. But she missed deleting all of them."

"That makes sense," I say. "Her brain is like mine and being consistent isn't the easiest thing. As least for me."

Dr. Tanaka stares at the screen for a moment. "Huh. It looks like she went from youngest to oldest."

Profe raises an eyebrow. "Is that youngest to oldest by the age of the cadaver or by the amount of time they spent out in the field?"

Dr. Tanaka squints at the screen again. "Time out in the field. Cadaver 072405, Mr. Gearhart, was the first one she infected, and we had just placed him out in the field. The last one she infected was Cadaver 072201, Mr. Hutchinson. He'd been out there the longest."

"What are you thinking, Frani?" Profe asks.

"Nothing that will make sense, most likely." Essie sighs.

Profe gives her a stern look, and she purses her lips.

I take a deep breath, trying to organize what I'm thinking so I don't start in the middle. "I think she was testing a hypothesis. She was seeing how much decomposition could take place before her bugs stopped being effective."

Profe and Dr. Tanaka look at each other, processing what I've said.

I chew on the inside of my mouth, still trying to sort

through the big idea that's forming in my head among all the different ideas setting off like firecrackers.

"The oldest," I say.

Essie groans and opens her mouth, but Profe shoots her another look and she stays quiet.

"Keep going," Benji says.

"What's the oldest cadaver we have out there in the field?" I ask, twisting the corner of my T-shirt between my fingers.

Profe thinks for a moment. "Cadaver 111403"

"Oh right, Winston!" I say. Biting my lip, my brain rockets through four separate thoughts. "It would have to be something a little younger. Not just bones. Definitely would still need a brain."

Dr. Tanaka clicks through some files on the computer. "Looks like that would be Cadaver 052201. Mr. Brady Kirby."

"Please tell me he wasn't a professional alligator wrestler or a circus trapeze artist," Benji groans.

"He was an accountant," Dr. Tanaka responds, narrowing his eyes at the information on the screen.

"So that's the plan? Go find Pilar's newest DUD and inject it with wrinkle-curing serum?" Benji asks.

Santiago looks at me and takes a deep breath. "But the . . . biology building? Is she taking . . . an extra credit class or something?"

I shake my head. "I think she's trying to duplicate what happened to you."

"How?" Benji asks.

"Is there a chance the biology building has snake venom? She could've stolen it. That way she can reanimate a cadaver with one of her bugs and also inject it with the venom. A recipe for a supercharged DUD," I suggest.

Dr. Tanaka nods. "The evidence suggests that she's probably created a new, stronger reanimated cadaver. We need to take care of it."

"Okay, team, here's what we're gonna do," Profe says, slipping the vial and a syringe into a small pouch. "First, we need to confirm that the cadaver we think Pilar might've infected, Mr. Kirby, is gone. If it is, I'll alert Captain Reynolds. I'll also contact the head of the biology department and ask her to check if there's any snake venom missing."

"Go, team?" Benji raises his fist in the air.

"This is so weird," Essie says, rolling her eyes.

I look at Santiago. "Are you up for this?"

The ice packs tucked into his clothes don't seem to be slowing down his decomposition anymore. His skin sags off his frame and his eyes look like they might roll back into his skull any second.

Santiago taps his finger on the table. His nail immediately snaps off. "Well . . . one last adventure."

Benji pats him lightly on the back. "We'll make sure it's a good one."

Dr. Tanaka grabs an iPad. "I've got the location of Cadaver 052201's plot out in the field on here."

"Let's go see if Mr. Kirby is still there," I say.

We march out of the lab and into the field. I trip three times over rocks and Benji has to grab my elbow. The summer sun beats down on us and I'm certain the ice packs we tucked into Santiago's clothes this morning melted immediately.

Passing a large live oak tree and a patch of mesquite bushes, we finally arrive at the location next to a clump of prickly pear cacti where Cadaver 052201 is supposed to be.

Except Mr. Kirby isn't there. The dirt is loose around a shallow hole in the ground and there's a small empty vial and a syringe lying at the edge.

I groan.

I've never felt so bad for being right before.

TWENTY-SIX

"WHERE COULD MR. Kirby possibly be?" Benji asks, crouching down and picking up a small rock from the ground.

"Better question: When we do find him, how much of a superpowered DUD are we going to be dealing with?" I ask.

Dr. Tanaka slips on some gloves and collects the vial and syringe from the ground, placing them in a red plastic bag.

"I don't think . . . he'll be that powerful," Santiago says. He stumbles slightly while standing. "I don't feel . . . that way."

"You've got a little more wear and tear on you. Even though Mr. Kirby is an older cadaver, he just popped out of the ground," I say, and then quickly realize I was less than polite. "Sorry."

Santiago shrugs. "You ever tried . . . to make cereal . . . but the milk was spoiled . . . and came out all chunky and smelly?"

I nod. "Yeah. Why?"

"I'm the spoiled milk."

I laugh and pat Santiago as gently as I can on the back as Profe calls Captain Reynolds on his phone, updating him on everything we've figured out.

"It's possible this cadaver might be a little stronger than the ones we've encountered before. We should've brought the tranquilizer guns out here as well. That way we could slow it down before injecting the Botox," Profe explains, slipping his phone back into his pocket.

"We can go get them!" Benji volunteers, enthusiastically raising his hand.

Dr. Tanaka points at him and raises his eyebrow. "Go get them. But don't use them."

"Dad, no offense, but you're like clouds at a fireworks show. Or rain at a baseball game." Benji smirks.

Dr. Tanaka shakes his head with a smile and waves us up the hill. We walk slowly so Santiago can keep up. There's really no hurry anyway since we have no idea where Pilar and her DUD sidekick could be.

I hear footsteps behind me and glance to see Essie following us, a scowl on her face. "I'm coming with you to make sure you don't get hurt. Or do anything stupid," she says.

"Full-time . . . job," Santiago wheezes. He tries to nudge me with his elbow, but his arm barely moves. "We're experts . . . at stupid."

When we finally get to the lab, my forehead is dripping with sweat and my shirt sticks to my back. Benji rushes over to the cabinet that holds the case with the tranquilizer guns. After grabbing three bottles of water from the small fridge Profe keeps next to his desk, we head back out into the field again.

I take a long sip of water from my bottle as Santiago stares at me.

"Do you want some?" I ask.

He slowly shakes his head. "I don't think . . . it would matter. Like a bucket . . . full of holes."

"It could use some perfume or something," Essie says, waving her hand in front of her nose.

"He's not an it," I tell her. "His name is Santiago."

"Whatever. At least you didn't get distracted twelve times before we even made it to the lab," Essie shoots back.

Benji leans close to Santiago. "Have I ever told you how thankful I am that I'm an only child?"

Santiago smiles. "Me too."

"Why are you even here? You hate this place," I tell Essie, stomping my foot on the ground.

She plants her hands on her hips. "Somebody has to make sure you don't mess everything up and get hurt. Do you know how many times I've been late to school because of you? Or how often I have to make dinner because you can't be trusted not to burn the entire kitchen down? All while you and Dad have your little bond over all this dead stuff. It's exhausting!"

I try to think of something to say, but my brain won't settle on just the right thing, which makes me angry because it feels like I'm proving Essie right.

"Be . . . quiet," Santiago says, his voice barely a whisper.

He's staring at Essie with narrowed eyes. His gray tongue juts from his mouth and licks his cracked lips.

Essie raises an eyebrow. "Excuse me?"

"She's your sister. . . . You should . . . be nicer."

Benji leans in toward Santiago. "I don't want to tell you what to do, man, but you're kind of poking the bear here."

Before Essie can say anything in response, a low growl fills the air. I look at Santiago but it's not coming from him.

The snarling swirls through the branches of the live oak tree we're standing under. I look down the hill and drop my water bottle.

Shuffling toward us, faster than I've ever seen Santiago or any of the other DUDs move, is Mr. Kirby. I stumble backward and trip over a cage on the ground covering another cadaver.

Benji helps me up, and we crouch next to the cage. Essie races behind a live oak tree and out of sight.

But Santiago stays with his feet planted firmly on the ground, facing Mr. Kirby as he barrels toward us.

"Santiago!" I hiss, not wanting to draw the superpowered

DUD's attention. "Move! Don't let him get to you."

I clench the sides of the cage in front of me and my finger goes straight into the leg of the cadaver underneath it. I grab Benji's arm and pull him up. We run toward a mesquite bush. Mr. Kirby snaps his gaze toward us and changes course.

Mr. Kirby snarls as he approaches. He's wearing a CTU T-shirt and sweatpants, no doubt put on him by Pilar. His eyes are red and his hair is completely gone. The gray skin on his arms is torn, revealing decomposed muscle underneath. And then I see why Mr. Kirby hasn't said anything, even though he's superpowered like Santiago.

His jaw is completely missing.

Essie screams. "Move!"

She snaps me from my trance, and I stop staring at Mr. Kirby. But he's still running straight toward me and Benji. A rock flies through the air and slams into the side of his head. His right ear falls off from the impact. His head snaps in Essie's direction, and her eyes grow wide.

He turns a few feet from us and runs toward Essie. But Santiago steps in his way, stumbling forward. He collides with Mr. Kirby, the sound more of a squelch than a crash. They tumble to the ground, Mr. Kirby falling on top of Santiago.

Benji pulls me toward the tree Essie is hiding behind. "Climb!" he shouts.

Essie stares up at the long winding branches of the live oak tree.

"You've got to be kidding," she says.

Mr. Kirby snarls and begins to pull himself off Santiago.

Essie looks at me. "Let's go," she says, yanking my arm.

I jump toward the lowest branch and grab it. Essie does the same and the branch creaks under our weight. We swing our bodies and wrap our legs around the branch, shifting until we can sit upright.

"Think it'll hold?" I ask Essie.

She doesn't answer, her hands gripping the bark of the tree with white knuckles.

Benji sprints below us toward the cadaver cage we'd crouched behind and grabs the tranquilizer case. He looks at the pile of body parts that is Mr. Kirby and Santiago.

Mr. Kirby stands and towers over Santiago. He has to be over six feet tall. Although most of his muscle has decomposed, it's obvious he was very imposing when he was alive, probably scaring people into doing their taxes correctly.

Benji hops up on the cadaver cage, but it's not enough to keep Mr. Kirby away since it's only two feet tall.

"Hey!" Benji shouts, holding the tranquilizer case above his head. "I'm gonna toss it."

I hold my arms up. "Go for it!"

Mr. Kirby snarls and growls, the sound coming from deep in his throat since the lower half of his face is gone.

He stumbles toward Benji, his arms outstretched and fingers curled unnaturally. Santiago tries to sit up, but his chest heaves and his eyes squeeze shut. He can barely move.

"Hurry!" Essie calls, waving her arms.

Benji grunts and launches the tranquilizer case in the air. It's headed straight for Essie. She reaches for it and loses her balance on the tree branch, toppling forward. I grab the back of her T-shirt and hold her steady just as she wraps her arms around the case. Her breath catches in her throat, and she looks at me.

"Thanks," she says, handing me the case.

The flying case distracted Mr. Kirby long enough for Benji to hop down from the cadaver cage and hide behind another mesquite bush. But now Mr. Kirby's head is snapping around, looking for something else to chase.

"We've got to keep him here," I tell Essie, loud enough so Benji can hear me too. "We can't let him run away. We have to shoot him with the tranquilizer gun."

Benji gives me a thumbs-up from behind the mesquite bush. I open the case and take out the tranquilizer gun. Removing one dart from the case, I insert it into the gun.

"Be careful. Have you ever used that before?" Essie asks, her eyebrow raised.

I bite my lip, thinking of the complete luck I had hitting Ms. Soto above the eye with a dart outside the football stadium. "Um, once?"

Mr. Kirby spots a squirrel perched on top of a cadaver cage down the hill and stumbles toward it. Benji hops out from behind the mesquite bush and waves his arms in the air.

"Hey, you reanimated meat sack! Over here!"

I aim the tranquilizer gun, trying to calm my breathing, but Mr. Kirby is reaching out toward the squirrel and moving away from me. Soon he'll be out of range.

Then something hits him in the gut, and he falls forward to his knees.

There's an arm lying on the ground.

Santiago sits up. His left arm is gone. He's trying to stand but his legs won't bend.

"Hurry, Frani! Shoot it!" Essie cries.

I snap my gaze away from Santiago and zero in on Mr. Kirby. Aiming as carefully as I can, I pull the trigger.

The dart flies through the air and slams into the back of Mr. Kirby's neck, the pink puff sticking out right below his hair. His shoulders heave three times and then he topples to the ground, face-first.

"We did it!" Benji cries. He runs over to me and Essie.

I stuff the tranquilizer gun back in its case and drop it down to Benji. Sliding my body down off the branch, I jump to the ground. Essie looks at me and bites her lip.

"It's okay," I tell her. "You can just hop down. It's not too far."

She launches herself off the branch and loses her balance when she hits the grass. I catch her and help her stand.

"Thanks," she mumbles.

We run over to Santiago. He's not moving.

"Are you okay?" I ask.

Santiago slowly shakes his head. "I've been in . . . better shape. Less like a puzzle . . . of body parts."

Benji walks over to Mr. Kirby and nudges him with his foot. When he doesn't respond, Benji reaches down and picks up the spare arm on the ground. He jogs back to us and holds the arm out to Santiago.

"I think this is yours," he says.

The hand on the arm is missing two fingers, and the bone at the elbow pokes through the skin.

"Not sure . . . this can be fixed," Santiago says.

I crouch down and examine Santiago. There's a bulge at his torso under his hoodie. It's one of his ribs.

"I'm sorry," I say, afraid to even touch him. "I don't know what we're gonna do."

Essie scuffs her feet in the grass and glances at Santiago. "Thanks," she says.

"What?" Santiago looks at her, taking the arm from Benji and laying it on his lap.

Essie takes a deep breath and crosses her arms. "I said thanks. You got in the way when that thing was running at me. I'm sorry you got demolished or whatever."

Santiago smiles. The skin on his bottom lip splits and creates a gash that goes down his chin.

"No problem," he says. "This was . . . fun."

TWENTY-SEVEN

THINGS USUALLY HAPPEN quickly in my brain, but they happen even faster after I shoot Mr. Kirby. Profe and Dr. Tanaka run up the hill to us, and they have Pilar in tow. She has long, deep scratches on her arms and a chunk of her hair has been yanked out above her left ear.

I crouch down next to Mr. Kirby and notice several black hairs wrapped around his fingers. The tips of his nails are tinged red.

Pilar's superpowered DUD must've turned on her.

I walk over to her and cross my arms as Profe calls Captain Reynolds.

"You should take her straight to the Cerro County police headquarters this time so there's no chance she can escape again and create DUDs. Although I'm not sure she wants to anymore," he tells the captain.

Pilar purses her lips.

"You're not going to stop, are you?" I ask her.

She narrows her eyes at me. "Oh, you know how it is, Frani Fran. Once we get something in our brain, we just can't let it go. It's how we are."

I shake my head. "Stop using your brain as an excuse. I used to do that. I'd blame Arañita for everything. But you know what? Just because she came up with an idea didn't mean I had to do it. I'm the one who's responsible in the end. You need to figure that out."

Pilar doesn't look at me. She's staring at Mr. Kirby. Her fingers tap on her leg and her foot bounces up and down. She's already calculating another experiment.

Once Profe is done talking to Captain Reynolds, he prepares a syringe and kneels down next to Mr. Kirby. He places the needle of the syringe to Mr. Kirby's temple. Santiago watches him carefully.

"That'll . . . do it?" he asks. "His brain . . . will stop?"

I sit down in the grass next to Santiago. He leans slightly against me, and I can feel the bones in his shoulder through his hoodie.

Profe nods. "Yes. This will stop his brain activity. He'll be a cadaver again."

Pressing the needle into Mr. Kirby's temple, Profe injects the dose of Botox. Once it's done, he slips the syringe into a red plastic bag from his backpack.

"Sir?" Santiago asks, his voice barely audible.

Profe looks at him.

Santiago's mouth opens and closes a few times, as if he's trying to find the air to speak.

"How many doses . . . do you have?" he finally says.

"What are you talking about?" I ask him.

Santiago turns his head slowly, his red eyes searching my face. "I think . . . this is it."

I look pleadingly at Profe. My stomach churns, and a lump presses in my throat. "There's really nothing we can do?"

Profe shakes his head. "This was never going to be a long-term thing. There's a natural order, and Pilar violated that."

I hear Pilar grunt behind me, but she doesn't say anything.

Profe walks over to Santiago and sits next to him on the grass. He places his hand gently on Santiago's leg. "I have one more dose in my bag. Is that what you want now?"

Santiago takes a deep breath, his throat wheezing, and nods.

I want to argue with him. My brain races through twenty different outlandish solutions for Santiago's predicament, but deep down I know none of them will work. Benji comes up behind me and sets his hand on my shoulder.

"Whatever you decide, we'll help you," he says to Santiago.

Essie clears her throat. "You deserve to make this decision yourself. Especially after everything that's happened to you against your will."

I give Essie a small smile, but I can't say anything yet. I just stare at Santiago's hand and wrap mine around it.

Santiago looks at Profe. "I can't . . . move. I think . . . it's time."

Profe pats Santiago's leg. He pulls his backpack over and removes another syringe and vial from it.

"One thing before . . . I go," Santiago says, looking at me.

"Anything," I quickly reply.

"Will you . . . write a letter?"

Dr. Tanaka hands me a notebook from his backpack. I take it and I turn to a clean page. "What do you want to say?"

It takes Santiago a while to tell me his letter, his words coming out in a slow whisper. But I carefully take down each and every one in my best handwriting.

Dear Ms. Salgado,

Thank you for looking for me. I'm okay now. I went on an adventure and made some friends. I'm the happiest I've been since I used to go fishing with

Abuelo. Don't worry about me. I'll be okay.

Thank you for seeing me.

Your student,

Santiago

"She teaches at my school," Essie tells Santiago. "I'll make sure she gets it."

"Thank you . . . for everything," he says.

Benji nudges him gently in the back. "We kinda had fun, didn't we?"

Santiago nods and smiles slightly. He seems to be fading, each movement more and more difficult.

Dr. Tanaka and Essie join us around Santiago.

He looks at each of us as Profe helps him lie back on the grass. I don't let go of his hand.

"Thank you," he says. "Thank you . . . all. For being . . . my family. Even for . . . a little bit."

Profe places his hand on Santiago's shoulder. "Of course. You deserved much more, but I'm thankful we could be here for you."

"I always wanted a brother," Benji says. His voice catches in his throat and he coughs. "Mostly so I could have help with chores. But I think we would've had fun defeating *Brain Basher 3*."

Essie fidgets and shrugs. "Believe it or not, you're less

annoying than this one here," she says, nudging me.

I blink several times, and tears start to stream down my face.

Santiago squeezes my hand. "I can't wait . . . to tell Abuelo . . . about you."

Profe moves the syringe closer to Santiago's temple, but I hold my hand up and stop him.

"You know," I say, my voice breaking, "there's no goodbye for the people we love. Not really. Our bodies may go back in the dirt, but there's no goodbye for our hearts."

Santiago smiles and squeezes my hand again. Then he nods slightly at Profe.

Working quickly, Profe injects Santiago with the syringe in his temple. He lays the needle on a red plastic bag and then places his hand on Santiago's forehead.

A small smile pulls at the corners of Santiago's mouth. Then his eyes close and he lies still.

I listen to the crickets chirping in the bushes and look up as a hawk circles overhead.

Essie takes my hand and squeezes it. I put my head on her shoulder and cry.

TWENTY-EIGHT

IT'S BEEN TWO weeks since the body farm became the "those shouldn't be up and walking around" farm. Seventh grade starts tomorrow. Somehow that's less frightening than anything that's happened recently.

"Hey, Santiago. Hey, Winston," I say, sitting down on the large limestone rock next to Winston's plot.

"I brought you my favorite candy," Benji says, placing three cherry Hi-Chews under a new marker next to Winston. It says OUR FRIEND SANTIAGO. ON TO THE NEXT ADVENTURE.

After Santiago died for the second time, Captain Reynolds decided it would be best to bury him at the body farm. There would be too much explaining to do otherwise. Essie gave Santiago's letter to Ms. Salgado at San Zavala High School. Captain Reynolds said that a couple of weeks later, Santiago's entry in the National Center for Missing and Exploited Children's database had been updated to "runaway."

But we knew the truth. We knew what happened to Santiago on the body farm. I wrote a new story all about him on the Story Stack so he wouldn't be forgotten. It's my most popular entry right now. Everyone thinks it's all made up, a story about zombies almost overtaking a college campus. But I wrote about how Santiago helped us solve a mystery and how he worked to round up the missing DUDs.

I wrote about my friend.

"You're not going to believe this, Santiago," I say, picking at my shoelace. "Essie made me breakfast this morning. And not in a 'I'm doing this so you don't burn the house down' way. In a nice way."

I look at the pile of dirt next to Santiago's marker. Grass is starting to grow through it.

I have so many questions I wish I could've asked him. I've even started writing a continuation to my Santiago entry on the Story Stack. I imagine what I think would've happened if he'd been able to keep working with us at the body farm. In my story, he's pretty much the best zombie assistant ever. I make sure he gets to have plenty of adventures, try all sorts of new foods, and learn so many new things.

Most of all, in my story, he's loved by his family.

"I wish you were here for the start of school," Benji says as he stares at the place where Santiago is buried. "I'm not that excited about being the new kid."

"At least we have each other. Maybe we'll have some of

the same classes," I tell him, nudging him with my elbow.

Benji nods. "That'll be so much better. Not having to eat lunch alone. Being able to ask someone where math class is so I don't accidentally walk into the girls' locker room. Not that I've ever done that before."

I start to imagine how Benji will react when he sees that if it weren't for him, I'd be eating stale cafeteria pizza alone. Or that he'll probably be the only person willing to be my lab partner in science class.

Will he still want to be friends with me? Will all those things finally make him decide I'm too weird to hang around with?

"So what are you gonna write about if we have to do one of those 'What I Did Last Summer' essays?" Benji asks, snapping me from my spiraling thoughts. "I'm definitely writing about all this. It'll probably win a Best Fiction Ever prize."

I laugh and shake my head. Benji just battled a squad of reanimated cadavers with me. I don't think I need to worry about how he'll react to me or seventh grade.

"Profe had me sit down and write out my goals for the school year. It was mostly 'don't be late,' 'don't interrupt people when they're talking,' and 'don't lose my cell phone,'" I tell Benji, picking a dandelion from the base of the rock we're sitting on and blowing its wispy petals in the air.

Profe and I took each of my goals and outlined all the

steps it would take for me to reach them. I was surprised when Essie sat down with us and helped.

"If you tell me what breakfast you're into lately, I can make sure it's ready for you. That way you won't get distracted by a million other things in the kitchen," she said, grabbing the list from Profe and writing down *Ready-made breakfast* under *Don't be late for school.*

She's probably trying to prevent another Disaster Day, but it feels good to have her on my team again.

I know I'll probably have trouble with my goals. I'll still miss the bus because I got distracted or lost track of what I was doing. I'm certain I'll blurt things out when I'm talking to someone because I'm afraid I'll forget what I was going to say. And I know that I'll most likely lose my cell phone a couple of times and not be able to picture where I last had it.

But that's okay. That's just how my brain works.

Profe already set up weekly visits for me with the school counselor so I could check in with her about my goals. He said that I could go see her if I ever felt overwhelmed or frustrated. I'll probably be seeing her a lot the first month of school, but I don't mind that.

If rounding up DUDs at the body farm showed me anything, it's that we all need a little help sometimes.

I wrap the end of my ponytail around my finger. "Essie said I should add 'don't talk about dead things so much,' but I left that off. Why should I hide what I'm interested in?"

“We should start a Dead Things club at school,” Benji suggests.

I laugh. “You know, that may not be the worst idea.”

I stand up from the rock and stretch, my back aching.

“Frani!” Profe calls from up the hill. “We’ve got another intake to process. Wanna help?”

I smile and raise my thumb in the air. Benji claps, a huge grin on his face.

“We’ll see you tomorrow, Santiago,” I say. “We’re gonna go on another adventure.”

AUTHOR'S NOTE

The Forensic Anthropology Research Facility (FARF) at Texas State University in San Marcos, Texas, serves as the inspiration for this book. The 26-acre facility is the largest of its kind and draws researchers and scientists from all over the world.

I first learned of this facility when I was leaving the grocery store and found that my car battery had died. I called a rideshare so that I could get home before the ice cream I'd bought melted. My driver told me he had just picked up a professor from the airport and driven him to FARF. I was so fascinated by the fact that I lived so close to such a unique facility, I started researching it right away.

Professors, students, and researchers at FARF learn about human decomposition and train in the search and recovery of human bodies. They also work with law enforcement and death investigators. All bodies at the body farm are donated from people who registered their bodies before they die. There is currently a list of one thousand people who have signed their bodies up for donation.

ACKNOWLEDGMENTS

Authors often write from personal experience, drawing from our past and present to inform our stories. While this book portrays my own experiences with ADHD, there is one element I'm pleased to say is entirely fictional and not based in my reality—Frani's relationship with her sister, Essie. My own sister, Heather, has always been my champion, lovingly guiding me and cheering me on. Thank you for pushing me, in ways only a big sister can, to be better. And thank you for letting me dogsit Jasper whenever I need a writing retreat.

Many thanks to Dr. Danny Wescott, director of the Forensic Anthropology Research Facility at Texas State University. He kindly answered all my questions and didn't bat an eye when I asked what would happen if one of the cadavers on the body farm disappeared.

No acknowledgments are ever complete without thanking my agent and friend, Stefanie Sanchez Von Borstel. We've been together for seven years now, and I can't imagine anyone better to guide my career. I'll always pick up the phone for you.

Thank you to Carolina Ortiz of HarperCollins for helping craft and fine-tune this story.

All my gratitude goes to the imaginative and incredible Eva Cabrera for bringing Frani's world to life with her amazing cover. Thank you to Corina Lupp for her spidery design. These are the interior pages of my creepy crawly dreams.

This introvert has been lucky enough to find loving friends who support me and cheer me on. I am forever grateful for Natalia, Lori, Amparo, Minh, Yaikira, and Ceci. May the group chats never be published!

True to form for a story that deals with ADHD, I experienced creative burnout while writing this book. So I have to give my thanks to the people and things who helped me recharge: BTS, *The Rose*, the McNay and Blanton art museums, the Florida Panthers hockey team, and all the amazing authors whose books I read to inspire me.

I wouldn't have a single book on the shelves without the love and support of my husband and son. Thank you for putting up with all the gross-out stories I excitedly told you during my research and please forgive me for forgetting that not everyone is as enthusiastic about decomposition as I am. I'm so blessed to have you both by my side.

And finally to my readers. We've come a long way together, haven't we? I hope you find refuge and a place to belong in my stories. Here's to more chaotic adventures in the future!